P9-DDX-670

THE LAUGHING MONSTERS

THE LAUGHING MONSTERS

DENIS JOHNSON

FARRAR, STRAUS AND GIROUX NEW YORK

Farrar, Straus and Giroux
18 West 18th Street, New York 10011

Printed in the United States of America
First edition, 2014

Library of Congress Cataloging-in-Publication Data
Johnson, Denis, 1949–
The laughing monsters : a novel / Denis Johnson.
pages cm
ISBN 978-0-374-28059-8 (hardback) — ISBN 978-0-374-70923-5 (ebook)
1. Political fiction. I. Title.

PS3560.O3745 L38 2014
813'.54—dc23

2014016983

Designed by Jonathan D. Lippincott

Farrar, Straus and Giroux books may be purchased for educational, business, or promotional use. For information on bulk purchases, please contact the Macmillan Corporate and Premium Sales Department at 1-800-221-7945, extension 5442, or write to specialmarkets@macmillan.com.

www.fsgbooks.com
www.twitter.com/fsgbooks • www.facebook.com/fsgbooks

10 9 8 7 6 5 4 3 2 1

For assistance way beyond the call of duty, the author thanks Michele Thompson.

For Charlie and Scout

ONE

Eleven years since my last visit and the Freetown airport still a shambles, one of those places where they wheel a staircase to the side of the plane and you step from European climate control immediately into the steam heat of West Africa. The shuttle to the terminal wasn't bad, but not air-conditioned.

Inside the building, the usual throng of fools. I studied the shining black faces, but I didn't see Michael's.

The PA spoke. Only the vowels came through. I called over the heads of the queue at the desk—"Did I hear a page for Mr. Nair?"

"No, sir. No," the man called back.

"Mr. Nair?"

"Nothing for such a name."

A man in a dark suit and necktie said, "Welcome, Mr. Naylor, to Sierra Leone," and helped me through the mess and chatted with me all through customs, which didn't take long, because I'm all carry-on. He helped me outside to a clean white car, a Honda Prelude. "And for me," he said, with a queasy-looking smile, "two hundred dollars." I gave him a couple of one-euro coins. "But, sir," he said, "it's not enough today, sir," and I told him to shut up.

The driver of the Honda wanted in the area of a million dollars. I said, "Spensy mohnee!" and his face fell when he saw I knew some Krio. We reached an arrangement in the dozens. He couldn't go any lower because his heart was broken, he told me, by the criminal cost of fuel.

At the ferry there was trouble—a woman with a fruit cart, policemen in sky-blue uniforms throwing her goods into the bay while she screamed as if they were drowning her children. It took three cops to drag her aside as our car thumped over the gangway. I got out and went to the rail to catch the wet breeze. On the shore the uniforms crossed their arms over their chests. One of them kicked over the woman's cart, now empty. Back and forth she marched, screaming. The scene grew smaller and smaller as the ferry pulled out into the bay, and I crossed the deck to watch Freetown coming at us, a mass of buildings, many of them crumbling, and all around them a multitude of shadows and muddy rags trudging God knows where, hunched forward over their empty bellies.

At the Freetown dock I recognized a man, a skinny old Euro named Horst, standing beside a hired car with his hand shading his eyes against the sunset, taking note of the new arrivals. As our vehicle passed him I slumped in my seat and turned my face away. After we'd passed, I kept an eye on him. He got back in his car without taking on any riders.

Horst . . . His first name was something like Cosmo but not Cosmo. Leo, Rollo. I couldn't remember.

I directed Emil, my driver, to the Papa Leone, as far as I knew the only place to go for steady electric power and a swimming pool. As we pulled under the hotel's awning another car came at us, swerved, recovered, sped past with a sign in its window—SPLENDID DRIVING SCHOOL. This resembled commerce, but I wasn't feeling the New Africa. I locked eyes with a young girl loitering right across the street, selling herself. Poor and dirty, and very pretty. And very young. I asked Emil how many kids he had. He said there were ten, but six of them died.

Emil tried to change my mind about the hotel, saying the place had become "very demoted." But inside the electric lights burned, and the spacious lobby smelled clean, or poisonous, depending on your opinion of certain chemicals, and everything looked fine. I'd heard the rebels had shot it out with the authorities in the hallways, but that had been a decade before, just after I'd run away, and I could see they'd patched it all up.

The clerk checked me in without a reservation, and then surprised me:

"Mr. Nair, a message."

Not from Michael—from the management, in purple ink, welcoming me to "the solution to all your problems," and crafted in a very fine hand. It was addressed "To Whom It May Concern." Clipped to it was a slip of paper, instructions for getting online. The desk clerk said the internet was down but not always. Maybe tonight.

I had a Nokia phone, and I assumed I could get a local SIM card somewhere, but—the clerk said—not at this hotel. For the moment, I was pretty well cut off.

Good enough. I didn't feel ready for Michael Adriko. He was probably here at the Papa in a room right above my head, but for all I knew he hadn't come back to the African continent and he wouldn't, he'd only lured me here in one of his incomprehensible efforts to be funny.

•

The room was small and held that same aroma saying, "All that you fear, we have killed." The bed was all right. On the nightstand, on a saucer, a white candle stood beside a red-and-blue box of matches.

I'd flown down from Amsterdam through London Heathrow. I'd lost only an hour and I felt no jet lag, only the need of a little repair. I splashed my face and hung a few things and took my computer gear, in its yellow canvas carrier-kit, downstairs to the poolside.

On the way I stopped to make an arrangement with the barman about a double whiskey. Then at a poolside table in an environment of artful plants and rocks, I ordered a sandwich and another drink.

A woman alone a couple of tables away pressed her hands together and bowed her face toward her fingertips and smiled. I greeted her:

"How d'body?"

"D'body no well," she said. "D'body need you."

I cracked my laptop and lit the screen. "Not tonight."

She didn't look in the least like a whore. She was probably just some woman who'd stopped in here to ease her feet and might as well seize a chance to sell her flesh. Right by the pool, meanwhile, a dance ensemble and percussionist had all found their spots, and the patrons got quiet. Suddenly I could smell the sea. The night sky was black, not a star visible. A crazy drumming started up.

Off-line, I wrote to Tina:

> I'm at the Papa Leone Hotel in Freetown. No sign of our old friend Michael.
>
> I'm at the poolside restaurant at night, where there's an African dance group, I think they're from the Kissi Chiefdom (they look like street people), doing a number that involves falling down, lighting things on fire, and banging on wild conga drums. Now one guy's sort of raping a pile of burning sticks with his clothes on and people at nearby tables are throwing money. Now he's rolling all around beside the swimming pool, embracing this sheaf of burning sticks, rolling over and over with it against his chest. It's a bunch of kindling about half his size, all ablaze. I'm only looking for food and drink, I had no idea we'd be entertained by a masochistic pyromaniac. Good Lord, Dear Baby Girl, I'm at an African hotel watching a guy in flames, and I'm a little drunk because I think in West Africa it's best always to be just a tiny bit that way, and the world is soft, and the night is soft, and I'm watching a guy

Across the large patio, Horst appeared and threaded himself toward me through the fire and haze. He was a tanned, dapper white-haired white man in a fishing vest with a thousand pockets and usually, I now remembered, tan walking shoes with white shoelaces, but I couldn't tell at the moment.

"Roland! It's you! I like the beard."

"C'est moi," I admitted.

"Did you see me at the quay? I saw you!" He sat down. "The beard gives you gravitas."

We bought each other a round. I told the barman, "You're quick," and tipped him a couple of euros. "The staff are efficient enough. Who says this place has gone downhill?"

"It's no longer a Sofitel."

"Who owns it?"

"The president, or one of his close companions."

"What's wrong with it?"

He pointed at my machine. "You won't get online."

I raised my glass to him. "So Horst is still coming around."

"I'm still a regular. About six months per year. But this time I've been kept home almost one full year, since last November. Eleven months."

The entertainment got too loud. I adjusted my screen and put my fingers on the keyboard. Rude of me. But I hadn't asked him to sit down.

"My wife is quite ill," he said, and he paused one second, and added, "terminal," with a sort of pride.

Meanwhile, two meters off, by the pool, the performer had set his shirt and pants on fire.

To Tina:

I saw a couple of US soldiers in weird uniforms at the desk when I checked in. This place is the only one in town that has electricity at night. It costs $145 a day to stay here.

Hey—the beard's coming off. It's no camouflage at all. I've already been recognized.

With the drumming and the whooping, who could talk? Still, Horst wouldn't let me off. He'd bought a couple of rounds, discussed his wife's disease . . . Time for questions. Beginning with Michael.

"What? Sorry. What?"

"I said to you: Michael is here."

"Michael who?"

"Come on!"

"Michael Adriko?"

"Come on!"

"Have you seen him? Where?"

"He's about."

"About where? Shit. Look. Horst. In a land of rumors, how many more do we need?"

"I haven't seen him personally."

"What would Michael be here for?"

"Diamonds. It's that simple."

"Diamonds aren't so simple anymore."

"Okay, but we're not after simplicity, Roland. We're after adventure. It's good for the soul and the mind and the bank balance."

"Diamonds are too risky these days."

"You want to smuggle heroin? The drugs racket is terrible.

It destroys the youth of a nation. And it's too cheap. A kilo of heroin nets you six thousand dollars US. A kilo of diamonds makes you a king."

To Tina I wrote: Show's over now. Everyone appears uninjured. The whole area smells like gasoline.

"What do you think?" Horst said.

"What I think is, Horst—I think they'll snitch you. They'll sell you diamonds and then they'll snitch you, you know that, because around here it's nothing but snitches."

Maybe he took my point, because he stopped his stuff while I wrote to Tina:

> I'm getting drunk with this asshole who used to be undercover Interpol. He looks far too old now to get paid for anything, but he still sounds like a cop. He calls me Roland like a cop.

At any point I might have asked his first name. Elmo?

Horst gave up, and we just drank. "Israel," he told me, "has six nuclear-tipped missiles raised from the silos and pointing at Iran. Sometime during the next US election period—boom-boom Teheran. And then it's tit for tat, that's the Muslim way, my friend. Radiation all around."

"They were saying that years ago."

"You don't want to go home. Within ten years it will be just like here, a bunch of rubble. But our rubble here isn't radioactive. But you won't believe me until you check it with a Geiger counter." The whiskey had washed away his European manner. He was a white-haired, red-faced, jolly elfin cannibal.

In the lobby we shook hands and said good night. "Of

course they'd *like* to snitch you," he said. He stood on his toes to get close to my left ear and whisper: "That's why you don't go back the way you came."

•

Later I lay in the dark holding my pocket radio against the very same ear, listening with the other for any sound of the hotel's generator starting. A headache attacked me. I struck a stinky match, lit the candle, opened the window. The batting of insects against the screen got so insistent I had to blow out the flame. The BBC reported that a big storm with 120-kilometer-per-hour winds had torn through the American states of Virginia, West Virginia, and Ohio, and three million homes had suffered an interruption in the flow of their electricity.

Here at the Papa Leone, the power came up. The television worked. CCTV, the Chinese cable network, broadcasting in English. I went back to the radio.

The phones in Freetown emit that English ring-ring! ring-ring! The caller speaks from the bottom of a well:

"Internet working!"

Working!—always a bit of a thrill. My machine lay beside me on the bed. I played with the buttons, added a PS to Tina:

> I drew cash on the travel account—5K US. Credit cards still aren't trusted. Exchange rate in 02 was 250 leones per euro, and the largest bill was 100 leones. You had to carry your cash in a shopping bag, and some used shoeboxes. Now they want dollars. They'll settle for euros. They hate their own money.

I sent my e-mails, and then waited, and then lost the internet connection.

The BBC show was *World Have Your Say*, and the subject was boring.

The walls ceased humming and all went black as the building's generator powered down, but not before I had a short reply from Tina:

Don't go back the way you came.

Suddenly I had it. Bruno. Bruno Horst.

•

Around three that morning I woke and dressed in slacks, shirt, and slippers, and followed my Nokia's flashlight down eight flights to the flickering lobby. Nobody around. While I stood in the candle glow among large shadows, the lights came on and the doors to both elevators opened and closed, opened and closed once more.

I found the night man asleep behind the desk and sent him out to find the girl I'd seen earlier. I watched while he crossed the street to where she slept on the warm tarmac. He looked one way, then the other, and waited, and finally nudged her with his toe.

I took an elevator upstairs, and in a few minutes he brought her up to my room and left her.

"You're welcome to use the shower," I said, and her face looked blank.

Fifteen years old, Ivoirian, not a word of English, spoke only French. Born in the bush, a navel the size of a walnut, tied by some aunt or older sister in a hut of twigs and mud.

She took a shower and came to me naked and wet.

I was glad she didn't know English. I could say whatever I wanted to her, and I did. Terrible things. All the things you can't say. Afterward I took her downstairs and got her a taxi, as if she had somewhere to go. I shut the car's door for her and heard the old driver saying even before he put it in gear: "You are a bad woman, you are a whore and a disgrace . . ." but she couldn't understand any of it.

•

I woke to the sound of a groundskeeper whisking dead mayflies from the walk below my balcony with a small broom. Around six it had rained hard for fifteen minutes, knocking insects out of the sky, and I call these mayflies for convenience, but they seemed half cockroach as well. Later, in the lobby, when I asked the concierge what sort of creature this was, he said, "In-seck."

Michael had called and left a message at the front desk. I asked the clerk, "Why didn't you put him through to the phone in my room?" and the young man scratched at the desk with his fingernail and examined his mark and seemed to forget the question until he said, "I don't know."

Michael wanted to meet me at 1600. At the Scanlon. That said a lot about his circumstances.

I wandered into the Papa's restaurant twenty minutes before the ten o'clock conclusion of the free buffet, the last person down to breakfast, and I found the staff thronging the metal warming pans, forking stuff onto plates for themselves. So this is what they eat, I thought, and by turning up with my own plate here I'm sort of fishing this fat banger sausage right out of somebody's mouth. You half-American pig. I took some fried potatoes too—the word for them is "Irish"—and then I couldn't eat, but I ate anyway, because they were watching me. Under their compassionate gazes I ate every crumb.

It was October, with temperatures around thirty Celsius most of the daytime, not unbearable in the shade, as always very humid. Right now we had a cool sea breeze, a few bright clouds in a blue sky, and a white sunshine that by noon would crash down like a hot anvil. The only other patron was a young American-looking guy in civilian clothing with a tattoo of a Viking's head on his forearm.

The power was up. American country music flowed through the PA speakers. I took the latter half of my coffee to a table near the television to catch the news on Chinese cable, but the local network was playing, and all I got was a commercial message from Guinness. In this advertisement, an older brother returns home to the African bush from his successful life in the city. He's drinking Guinness Draught with his younger brother in the sentimental glow of lamps they don't actually possess in the bush. Big-city brother hands little bush brother a bus ticket: "Are you ready to drink at the table of men?" The young one takes it with gratitude and determination, saying, "Yes!" The announcer speaks like God:

"Guinness. Reach for greatness."

•

After breakfast I went out front with my computer kit belted to my chest like a baby carrier. Sweat pressed through my shirt, but the kit was waterproof.

The only car out front had its bonnet raised. A few

young men waited astride their okadas, that is, motorcycles of the smallest kind, 90cc jobs, for the most part. I chose one called Boxer, a Chinese brand. "Boxer-man. Do you know the Indian market? Elephant market?"

"Elephant!" he cried. "Let's go!" He slapped the seat behind him, and I got on, and we zoomed toward the Indian market over streets still muddy and slick from last night's downpour, lurching and dodging, missing the rut, missing the pothole, missing the pedestrian, the bicycle, the huge devouring face of the oncoming truck—missing them all at once, and over and over. On arrival at the market with its mural depicting Ganesha, Hindu lord of knowledge and fire, I felt more alive but also murdered.

The elephant-faced god remained, but Ganesha Market had a new title—Y2K Supermarket.

"I'm waiting for you," my pilot told me.

"No. Finish," I said, but I knew he'd wait.

I left the Boxer at the front entrance and went out by the side. I believe in the underworld they call this maneuver the double-door.

Outside again I found a small lane full of shops, but I didn't know where I was. I made for the bigger street to my left, walked into it, was almost struck down, whirled this way by an okada rider, that way by a bicycle. I'd lost my rhythm for this environment, and now I was miffed with the traffic as well as hot from walking, and I was lost. For forty-five minutes I blundered among nameless mud-splashed avenues before I found the one I wanted and the little establishment with its hoarding: ELVIS DOCUMENTS.

Three solar panels lay on straw mats in the dirt walkway where people had to step around them. The hoarding read,

"Offers: photocopying, binding, typing, sealing, receipt/invoice books, computer training."

Inside, a man sat at his desk amid the tools of his livelihood—a camera on a tripod, a bulky photocopier, a couple of computers—all tangled in power cords.

He rose from his office chair, a leather swivel model missing its casters, and said, "Welcome. How can I be of service?" And then he said, "Ach!" as if he'd swallowed a seed. "It's Roland Nair."

And it was Mohammed Kallon. It didn't seem possible. I had to look twice.

"Where's Elvis?"

"Elvis? I forget."

"But you remember me. And I remember you."

He looked sad, also frightened, and made his face smile. White teeth, black skin, unhealthy yellow eyeballs. He wore a white shirt, brown slacks cinched with a shiny black plastic belt. Plastic house slippers instead of shoes.

"What's the problem here, Mohammed? Your store smells like a toilet."

"Are we going to quarrel?"

I didn't answer.

Everything was visible in his face—in the smile, the teary eyes. "We're on the same side now, Roland, because in the time of peace, you know, there can be only one side." He opened for me a folding chair beside his desk while he resumed his swivel. "I might have known you were in Freetown."

I didn't sit. "Why?"

"Because Michael Adriko is here. I saw him. The deserter."

"You call Michael a deserter?"

"Hah!"

"If he's a deserter, then call me a deserter too."

"Hah!"

I felt irritated, ready to argue. Mohammed was still a good interrogator. "Listen," I said, "Michael's not from any of these Leonean clans, any of the chiefdoms. I think he's originally from Uganda. So—if he left here suddenly back then, he didn't desert."

"Can't you sit down to talk?"

"Bruno Horst is around."

"I do believe it. So are you."

"Is he working for one of the outfits?"

"How would I know?"

"I don't know how you'd know. But you'd know."

"And who does Roland Nair work for?"

"Just call me Nair. Nair is in Freetown strictly on personal business. And it really does stink in here."

"Who do you work for?"

I shrugged.

"Anyone. As usual," he said.

I wasn't a torturer. I'd never stood ankle-deep in the fluids of my victims . . . "I can't imagine how you ended up here," I told him. "You're all wrong for this."

"Holy cow! All wrong for what?"

"You're a dirty player."

Mohammed had lost his smile. "I hear the pot saying to the kettle, 'You are black.' Do you know that expression?"

He had a point. "All right," I said, "we're both black," and it struck me as funny.

Mohammed found his smile again. "Nair, I don't want to get off on the wrong foot after so long a time, honestly—

because it's almost the moment when you take me to lunch!"

"Lunch isn't out of the question," I said. "But first give me a few minutes with your computers."

"None of them are working."

"The computers downstairs."

"There's no downstairs." He was a terrible liar. I stared until he understood. "Bloody hell!"

"Let's have a look inside your closet."

"Every day brings new surprises!" He looked as if he'd eaten something evil and delicious. "You're with NIIA?"

"Let's follow the protocol." The protocol called for his getting out of my way.

He sat back down and busied himself with a pile of receipts, bursting with a silly, private glee, while I went across the space to his mop closet, which stood open and which also served as a toilet, with a slop-bucket covered by a wooden board and a roll of brownish paper on the floor beside it. That accounted for the stench in the place.

I consulted the readout on my coder, a unit that fits on a key chain. The eight-digit code changes every ninety seconds. I entered the closet and shut the door behind me, and by the glow of my Nokia I moved aside a patch on the rear wall and keyed the digits into the interlock and pushed the wall open and went down the metal stairs as the panel clicked shut behind me without my assistance.

Here the four lights were burning.

I'd entered this sunken place more than once, long ago. It had been built to American standards, not in meters, but in feet: ten by sixteen in area, with concrete walls eight feet in height, and one dozen metal stair steps leading down. A battery bank in a wire cage bolted to the concrete floor, an electric bulb in another such cage in each of the concrete walls. A desk, a chair, both metal, both bolted down. On the desk, two machines—much smaller units than we'd used a dozen years before.

I sat down and took from my carrier-kit an accessory disguised as a cigarette lighter, a NATO-issued device similar to a USB stick, with the algorithms built in. It actually makes a flame. I held it to my face and scanned my iris and stuck it into the side of the machine in front of me and powered up and logged on. Through the NATO Intel proxy I sent a Nothing To Report—but I sent it twice, which warned Tina to expect a message at her personal e-address. For this exchange Tina would know to shelve the military algorithms. We used PGP encryption. As the name promised, it's pretty good protection.

I logged off of NIIA and attached my own keyboard to the console and went through the moves and established a Virtual Private Network and sent:

> Get file 3TimothyA for me. Your NEMCO password will work.

Nothing now but the sound of my breath and the prayers of three small cooling fans. The fans cooled the units, not the user. I wiped my face and neck with my kerchief. It came away drenched. My breath came faster and faster. My Nokia's clock showed a bit after 1300—noon in Amsterdam. I hadn't allowed time for getting lost. Tina might have gone to lunch. It irked me that I couldn't slow my breath.

But Tina was at her desk, and she was ready. I sent: "I'm ready for those dirty pictures."

Within two minutes it was done.

I believe that by making this transaction the two of us risked life sentences. But only one of us knew it. Like anyone in the field of intelligence, Tina asked no questions. Besides, she loved me.

I came up the stairs and into Elvis Documents with my kit clutched against my chest, as if it held the goods, but it didn't. A Cruzer device snugged in the waistline seam of my trousers held the goods.

Mohammed waited in his broken chair, his gaze fixed studiously in another direction.

"Let's eat," I said.

•

We ate down the street at the Paradi. Decent Indian fare.

During the late nineties and for a few years after, when this place had drawn the interest of the media, Kallon had worked as a stringer for the AP and as a CIA informant, and then the CIA had levered him into the Leonean secret service to inform from down in the nasty heart of things, and he had hurt a lot of people. And now he'd got himself a job with NATO.

That the CIA once ran Mohammed Kallon was, I acknowledge, my own supposition, prompted merely by my sharp nose for a certain perfume. Snitches stink.

I let Kallon order for both of us while I went to the men's lavatory. I slipped shut the lock and took my passport from my shirt pocket and the Cruzer from the seam in my trousers. I felt desperate to be rid of it. Cowardly—but the situation felt all too new.

Normally I carry my passport in a ziplock plastic bag. I removed the passport from the bag and replaced it with the Cruzer, wound the Cruzer tightly in the plastic, and looked for a hiding place.

The toilets, two of them, were set into the floor, each with a foot pedal for flushing. I examined the tiles on all four walls, fiddled with the mirror, ran my fingers around the windowsill. I tried lifting the posts of the divider between the two toilets—one came loose from the floor. With my finger I scratched a delve at the bottom of its hole, dropped the tiny package in, and replaced the post to cover it.

For the sake of realism, I pressed the pedal on one of the toilets. It didn't flush. The other one sprayed my shoe. I washed my hands at the sink and rejoined Mohammed Kallon.

Over lunch we talked about nothing really, except when I asked him outright, "What's going on?" and he said, "Michael Adriko is going on."

•

Having nowhere else to be, I arrived an hour early at the Scanlon, a hotel more central to Freetown than the better ones. When the region had drawn journalists, this was where many of them had lodged, a four-story place sunk in the diesel fumes and, when the weather was dry, in the hovering dust.

Inside the doors it was mute and dim—no power at the moment please sir—but crowded with souls. In the middle of the lobby stood a figure in a two-piece jogging suit of royal purple velour, a large man with a bald, chocolate, bullet-shaped head, which he wagged from side to side as he blew his nose loudly and violently into a white hand towel. People were either staring or making sure they didn't. This was Michael Adriko.

Michael folded his towel and draped it over his shoulder as I came to him. Though we had an appointment in an hour, he seemed to take my appearance here as some kind of setback, and his first word to me was, "*What*-what." Michael often uses this expression. It serves in any number of ways. A blanket translation would be "Bloody hell."

"Thanks for meeting me at the airport."

"I was there! Where were you? I watched everybody getting off the plane and I never saw you. I swear it!" He always lies.

He put out his monumental hand and gave mine a gentle shake, with a finger-snap.

"For goodness' sake, Nair, your beard is gray!"

"And my hair is still black as a raven's."

"Do ravens have beards?" He had his feet under him now. "I like it." Before I could stop him, he reached out and touched it. "How old are you?"

"Too close to forty to talk about."

"Thirty-nine?"

"Thirty-eight."

"Same as me! No. Wait. I'm thirty-seven."

"You're thirty-six."

"You're right," he said. "When did I stop counting?"

"Michael, you've got an American accent. I can't believe it."

"And I can't believe you bring a lovely full beard to the tropics."

"It's coming off right away."

"So is my accent," he said and turned to the waiter and spoke in thick Krio I couldn't follow, but I got the impression at least one of us was getting a chicken sandwich.

I asked the clerk if a barber was available, and he shook his head and told me, "Such a person does not exist."

I asked Michael, "Do you still carry your clippers?"

Smiling widely, he caressed his baldness. "I'm always groomed. Send the sandwich to my room," he told the clerk. "Two three zero."

"I know your room," the clerk said.

"Come, Nair. Let's chop it down with the clippers. You'll feel younger. Come. Come." Michael was moving off, calling over his shoulder to the desk clerk, "Also bottled water!" Looking backward, he collided with a striking woman—African, light-skinned—who'd tacked a bit, it seemed to me, in order to arrange the collision. He looked down at her and said, "*What*-what," and it was plain they were friends, and more.

It didn't surprise me she was beautiful, also young—not long out of university, I guessed. Such women succumbed to Michael quickly, and soon moved on.

She wore relief-worker or safari garb, the khaki cargo pants and fishing vest and light, sturdy hiking shoes. On this basis, I misjudged her. Really, that's all it was—I judged her according to her clothes, and the judgment was false. But the first impression was strong.

Michael looked put out with her. "Everybody's here at once."

"Not for long—I'm off exploring." She sounded American.

"Exploring where?" He was smiling, but he didn't like it.

"I'm looking for postcards."

I said, "You'll have to go to the Papa for that."

"Yes, the Papa Leone Hotel," Michael explained, "but it's too far."

"All right, I'll take a car."

Michael sighed.

"Don't pout," she said. "I'll be back in an hour."

"Wait. Meet my friend Roland Nair. This is Davidia St. Claire."

"Another friend? Everybody's his friend." Davidia St. Claire was speaking to me. "Did he say Olin?"

"My given name is Roland, but I never use it. Please call me Nair."

"Nair is better," Michael informed her. "It's sharper. Look," he went on, "at the Papa, get your nails done or something, kill some time, and let's all meet at the Bawarchi for dinner—early dinner, six p.m. We all should know each other, because Nair is my closest friend."

I said, "He saved my life."

"Oui?" Her eyebrows went up.

Michael said, "C'est vrai."

"More than once," I said.

"Three times."

"He kept me alive on a daily basis," I said, and his woman looked me over—as if I explained something she'd wondered about, that kind of look, and I didn't understand it. I said, "Are you Ivoirian?"

It made her laugh. "Who, me?"

"I thought because of the French."

"That's just for fun. I'm a Colorado girl."

"I'm half American myself," I said. I offered my hand. She laid two fingers on my wrist and seemed to watch my face as if to gauge the effect of her touch, which stirred me, in fact, like an anthem. She looked very directly into my eyes and said, "Hello."

And then, "Goodbye."

•

In room 230 I noticed a rollerbag I judged not quite in Michael's style, but nothing that clearly said the woman Davidia slept here.

Michael flipped the wall switch. "Still no power!" He went to the dresser, opened a drawer, and turned to me gripping a braided leather whip about a meter in length, knotted at the narrow end. He grasped its handle and pulled out a dagger. "Nobody will know about my blade!"

"But, Michael—they'll know about your whip."

"Well, let them know at least something. It's fair to be warned. Look how sharp. I could shave your beard with this."

"Show me to the clippers, please."

While I ran down the battery on his clippers at the sink, doing my best by the light through the small window, Michael cleaned his teeth, working away with a brush from whose other end a small spider dangled and swung.

There was another toothbrush sticking out of a water glass, and a tube of facial cream, and two kinds of deodorant. "Tell me your friend's name again."

He spat in the sink and said, "I've got a million friends,"

just like an American. "Look!" he cried. "It's Roland Nair emerging from the bush." He resumed his brushing—still talking, foaming at the mouth. "You have gray in the beard, but not on your head."

"A couple of days with you should fix that." I spoke to his reflection, side by side with my own.

I am Scandinavian but have black hair and gray eyes, or blue, according to the environment. If I wanted my appearance to impress, I'd stay away from the sun and keep a very white complexion to go with my raven locks, that would be my look. But I like the sun on my face, even in the tropics.

Michael has handsome features, a brief, aquiline nose, high cheekbones, wide, inquiring eyes—like one of those Ethiopian models—and as for his lips, I can't say. You'd have to follow him for days to get a look at his mouth in repose. Always laughing, never finished talking. A hefty, muscular frame, but with an angular grace. You know what I mean: not a thug. Still—lethal. I'd never seen him being lethal, but in 2004 on the Kabul–Kandahar road somebody shot at us, and he told me to stay down and went over a hill, and there was more shooting, and soon—none. And then he came back over the hill and said, "I just killed two people," and we went on.

Once he showed me a photograph, a little boy with Michael Adriko's face, his hand in the hand of a man he said was his father. Michael's father had Arab blood apparent in his features, and so Michael—well, there's a dash of cream in the coffee, invisible to me, but obvious to his fellow Africans. Sometimes he introduced me to them as his brother. As far as I could tell, he was never disbelieved.

He stroked his teeth with vigor. The spider whipped

around on its strand. He rinsed his brush and the spider was gone.

Now he watched me comb my hair. I think it fascinated him because he was bald. He laughed. "Your vanity doesn't make you look more lovely. It only makes you look more vain." At that moment, the ceiling fixture flickered to life. "Power's back. Let's see the news."

He sat on the bed and punched buttons on the television's wand, pushing the device toward the screen as if to toss the signal at it. "News. News. News." Al Jazeera had sports. The soccer scores. He settled for Nigerian cable, some sort of amateur singing competition, and then he untied his very clean red jogging shoes and kicked them off and set about massaging both feet, each with one hand. Vivid yellow socks.

"Michael—"

Michael laughed at the television.

"Michael, it's time you told me something. You contact me, you get me down here—"

"You contacted me! You said, What's going on, I said, Come down to SL and I'll show you a plan."

"Don't *show* me the plan. *Tell* me the plan."

But I'd lost him. He watched the screen with his mouth half open, his hands clutching his feet. The commercial ad from Guinness, the two black brothers, the bus ticket out of the bush . . . By the power brewed into this drink big-city brother frees his sibling from a curse that neither of them understands, and side by side they set out for the Kingdom of Civilization. Michael's eyes glistened and he smiled a wide, tight smile. I'd often seen him driven to tears—this was what it looked like. Something had caught him by the heart. Brother for brother, reaching for greatness. Michael was moved. Michael was weeping.

As quickly as the ad was over he leapt into the bathroom, splashed his face at the sink, blew his nose into the hand towel, loomed in the doorway.

"Here's the plan: I am a new man, and I plan to do what a new man does."

Now he stood in the middle of the room, offering me tomorrow in his two outstretched hands. "Do you want a plan? I'm just going to give you results. You'll live like a king. A compound by the beach. Fifty men with AKs to guard you. The villagers come to you for everything. They bring their daughters, twelve years old—virgins, Nair, no AIDS from these girls. You'll have a new one every night. Five hundred men in your militia. You know you want it. They dance at night, a big bonfire, and the magic men come and stretch their arms to the length of a python, and change into all kinds of animals, and drums pounding, and naked dancers, all just for you, Nair! We want it. That's what we want. And you know it's here. There's no place else on earth where we can have it."

"This land of chaos, despair—"

"And in the midst of it, we make ourselves unreachable. A man can choose a valley, one with narrow entrances—defensible entries—and claim it as his nation, like Rhodes in Rhodesia—"

"I can't believe I hear a black man talking like this."

"We'll have the politicians kissing our feet. Every four years we'll assassinate the president."

"The same president?"

"It's term limits! We'll be the ones controlling that."

"How many men with AKs?"

"How many did I say? A thousand. Nair, I'll come around on my launch on Sundays. Run it up onto the sand of your protected beach. Our children will play together. Our wives will be fat. We'll play chess and plan campaigns."

"You don't play chess."

"You haven't seen me for seven years."

"Man—you don't play chess."

He looked at me, wounded. So naked in his face. "That's why it has to be you. You're the one who knows those games."

"And your games too, right?"

"It has to be you."

I said, "This better not be about diamonds."

"Not diamonds. Not this time. This time we concern ourselves with metals and minerals."

"And aren't diamonds actually minerals?"

"This is why I can never make a point," Michael said, "because you query the details like some kind of master interrogator."

"Sorry. Is it gold, then?"

"I tell you now: Stay away from the gold here, unless I say otherwise. The gold around here is fake. You'd see that the minute you looked at a kilo bar of it—but by the time they give you a look, you're already in a dark place with bad people."

"I'll wait for your signal."

He sat beside me on the bed and placed a hand on my shoulder. "I want you to understand me. I have this mapped from point A to point Z. And, Nair—point Z is going to be marvelous. Did I ever tell you about the time I saved the Ghanaian president's life?"

It made me uncomfortable when he sat so close, but it was just an African thing. I said, "Michael, what about the girl? Who is she to you?"

"She's American."

"She told me that herself."

"I heard her telling you."

"Who is she, Michael?"

"More will be revealed."

This was his style, his tiresome, unchangeable way. Information was an onion, to be peeled back in layers.

"What about you? What's your passport?"

"Ghana," he said, and he didn't look happy about it. "Ghana will always welcome me."

I shrugged away his heavy hand and got up. "Enough of Michael's nonsense. Let's get a drink."

"Prior to sixteen hundred," he said, "I drink only bottled water."

"As they say, it's sixteen hundred somewhere." I checked my phone. "Here, as a matter of fact."

"I stink! Get out while I shower."

Looking down at him now—"Final question: What about Congo gold?"

"Nair!—you're so far ahead of me."

"If I was ahead of you, I'd know what I'm doing in Freetown instead of Congo, where all the gold is."

"The important thing is that you came without knowing why."

"I know why I came."

"But not why I asked you. You came without an explanation."

"You'd only lie to me, Michael."

"For security purposes, perhaps. Yes. For your protection in transit. But we're friends. We don't lie to each other."

He believed it.

•

As I made for the elevator, the lights died in the hallway. I took the stairs. Candles at the front desk, in the lobby, the big dining room. In the bar, the smell of burning paraffin, the stench of cologne overlying human musk. Voices from the dark—laughter—candlelit smiles. I ordered a martini, and it tasted just like one.

Tina strayed into my mind. I drank quickly and ordered another.

Why hadn't I simply loaded the goods into my Cruzer in Amsterdam, and left Tina out of things? That seemed simple enough—now. But I'd been sent here to Freetown on an NIIA errand, and I had no idea what sort of last-minute scrutiny the powers might have authorized. Anything at all seemed possible, including my being called aside at airport security and confronted with a couple of NIIA comptrollers donning latex gloves. Afraid of some kind of search, I'd made Tina some kind of patsy.

After I drained the second glass and ate the second olive—really, all would be well. Many people keep watch. Nobody sees. It takes a great deal to waken their curiosity. NATO, the UN, the UK, the US—poker-faced, soft-spoken bureaucratic pandemonium. They're mad, they're blind, they're heedless, and not one of them cares, not one of them.

I could have reasoned all this out from the start. But I'm a coward, and I couldn't bear living alone in the abyss. Therefore Tina, unaware, lived in it beside me.

Perhaps Tina and I would be married on my return, after I'd met my contact and sold the goods and made money enough for several honeymoons, and after I'd been relieved of my current duty, which was to report on the activities and, if possible, the intentions of Michael Adriko.

•

From half the distance down into my third martini, I heard Michael's voice in the lobby—"What happened to my sandwich?"

The desk clerk followed him. "It's coming to the room, sir."

"Send it to the bar, will you?"

He took the vacant stool beside mine and ordered a Guinness. I said, "Really? Guinness?"

"Guinness is good for you. Let's sit alone."

I joined him at a table with my martini. Two more sips, and I was ready to take him on.

"Talk to me, Miguel. Talk, or I walk."

"I'm here to talk," he said. "We're talking." But all he did with his mouth was pull on his beer.

"This place is a dump. What's wrong with the Papa Leone?"

"Too many people know me there."

"Right. You're broke."

"I'm on a budget. Is that dishonorable?"

"It's troubling."

"Why trouble yourself? Is it really your problem?"

"It is if I'm in business with you, because I'll end up living in this hovel. I can't run back and forth."

"That's your choice, Nair. Don't blame me."

"*Am* I in business with you?"

"That's also your choice."

I took a breath and counted to five. I released a delirious sigh. "What about the girl? Is she with us?"

"I met her in Colorado."

"Congratulations."

"Thanks. I'm a lucky man."

"Who is she?"

"More will be revealed." A lighter flared across the room, somebody starting a cigarette in a group of five white men. Michael cocked his head in that direction, not looking there, his face full of conspiracy. "Now, who are these fellows?"

"Pilots. Russian. They work for the charter outfits."

"They don't look like civilian pilots. They're all young, all fit. Why doesn't at least one of them have a beer belly? Look at the haircuts—regulation."

"All right, very good. Who are they?"

Suddenly he stood up and strode over to their table. He spoke. They replied, and he came back with an unlit cigarette between his teeth and sat down again. "It's a Rothmans," he said. "Australian."

"You're still smoking?"

"Now and then. But everything in moderation." He took up the candle between us and lit his Rothmans and sat back and blew smoke over my head. "Nair, I've got people on my trail."

"These guys?"

"It could be anyone."

"Are you in trouble? What's your situation?"

"I'll fill you in eventually."

"Stop it! Jesus!" I was the loudest one in the room. I

lowered my tone, but I leaned in to his face. "I expected you to be dealing with the big men. Moving money around. Dispensing government contracts, you know? Contracts, not contraband. Diverted aid, siphoned oil revenue, that kind of thing. Money, Michael. Money. Not pebbles and powders."

"Don't let your speech get so strong, mate. There's plenty of time for plenty of developments. Let's enjoy the moment." He mashed his cigarette in the candle's dish and looked away and entered a personal silence.

You had to be careful with him. For hurt feelings, Michael would stop the whole show.

I waited him out. It never took long.

"It's been seven years since we saw each other, Nair. I'm thirty-six years old now. I'm changed, I'm different. I'm new." He turned toward me fully and placed two clenched fists on the table as if in evidence of his newness. "I left Afghanistan four years ago. I underwent training for two years at Fort Bragg, in North Carolina, after which I was transferred to Fort Carson, in Colorado. At Fort Carson I worked as a trainer for internationals, mostly from South America, sometimes from the Middle East. They were confined to the post, and whenever I was part of the training team for an international group, I was also kept on the grounds. Between groups, yes, I could go into town in civilian clothes. On the post I wore a US Army uniform with a sergeant's hash marks. But I was not in the US Army."

A waiter came with a sandwich on a plate. Michael ignored him. He set it on the table. Michael ignored it.

"They promised me permanent US residency, Nair. They lied. They told me I was on a path to US citizenship. They lied. They said I would enter the US Army as an officer and go as far as my talents could take me. They lied."

He waited for comment. I provided none. The white men across the room were drinking like Russians. They laughed like Russians.

"Listen to me, Nair. I can build you a bomb. Just give me five minutes, I hardly have to move from this spot. Just bring me matches, Christmas lights, and sugar. I can shoot a man from one thousand meters. I've done it. I am a man of courage and discipline, and the reward for that is becoming a thug for hire. A goon, a pawn, a cog in a robot who is programmed only to tell you lies."

"Sure. We're all getting older and wiser. That's sort of my point."

"I've looked at every opportunity for changing my situation, and I've chosen the best one."

"Give me a piece of the plan. Anything."

"First of all," he said, "we'll go to Uganda for my wedding."

"Oh, God. Should I feel somewhat enlightened, or further confused?"

"Right. I'm engaged."

"Not for the first time."

"But for the last. I told you—I'm a new man."

"Is that what I'm here for? And nothing else?"

"It's important that we keep things need-to-know and take things one step at a time. Nair, please, you've got to trust me. Remember—once or twice, didn't we make a lot of money?"

"We made a lot of money for guys in their twenties.

Now we're grown-ups. We should be getting rich. Are you asking me to settle for less?"

"I'm not asking you to settle for less." He gathered himself, so to speak, around his bottle of Guinness, and went to his depths to collect his words. "Here is my promise to you: we are going to get rich."

His eyes were steady. I believed him. Or anyway I was tired, tired of the struggle to disbelieve. "Good enough," I said.

"So now, let's go. Let's have some dinner with my fiancée."

As we rose from our seats, I took in the group of possible Russians—now Michael had me doing it—all of them youngish, poised, and trim. I heard one say, "Are ya lovin' it!"

Michael left his sandwich. I drained my glass and surrendered to the hour. After all, I was getting paid for this.

•

As soon as we'd ordered our drinks at the Bawarchi—we'd come early; Davidia hadn't arrived—Michael started picking at a point. "Who contacted who?"

"I had your address at Fort Carson, so you must have contacted me first, or I wouldn't have known your whereabouts."

"Yes, yes—but after more than a year of silence between us, I had a letter from you that was forwarded from Fort Carson at the beginning of August."

"Forwarded to what location?"

"And then I answered you, and I said, 'Come to beautiful Sierra Leone!' "

"Maybe this time around, I contacted you first. Is any of this important?"

"Everything's important."

Judging by the throng of Europeans, we could expect good food here. It was a spacious Indian place on the outskirts of town, on the beach—open-air, excepting a thatched roof—with a cooling sea breeze and the surf washing softly within earshot. The beach was fine white damp sand, like table salt. In fifteen minutes it would be too dark to make it out.

Michael's suspicions touched everyone. Now he pointed out a middle-aged Euro at the bar. "CIA. I know him."

"I can only see his back."

"He was the head of the skeleton staff at the embassy in Monrovia. I knew him then."

"You? When?"

"When Charles Taylor held the East."

"You would have been—thirteen? Twelve?"

His face came under a cloud. "You don't know about my life."

In an instant the day ended, night came down, and the many voices around us, for the space of ten seconds, went quiet. A few hundred meters away the buildings began, but not a single light shone from the powerless city, and the outcry coming from the void wasn't so much from horns and engines, but rather more from humans and their despairing animals. Meanwhile, waiters went from table to table lighting tapers in tall glass chimneys.

And as soon as they'd made everything right, Davidia St. Claire entered the scene, slender, elegant, wearing an African dress. She had the usual effect of one of Michael's women. He wouldn't have had one who didn't. Even in the Third World he managed to find them, at fashion shows and photo shoots, at diplomatic cocktail parties—at church. The gazes followed behind her as if she swept them along with her hands.

Standing up for her, I knocked my chair over backward. Michael, sitting, extended his foot and caught it with his toe, and I was able to set it right before it clattered to the slate floor.

She laughed. "That's quite an act."

"In honor of your dress," Michael said. I held her chair for her, and he added, "Nair will hold your chair."

"I just bought it at the shop at the Papa Leone. It's from the Tisio Valley." She modeled for us, turning this way and that. The dress was mostly white, with a floral pattern, perhaps red—it was hard to say by candlelight—ankle-length, sleeveless and low cut and soft and clinging. I was aware, everybody was aware, of her arms and hands, and the insteps of her sandaled feet, and her toes. She dropped her shopping bag and sat down and smiled.

"It's almost as wonderful as you." Michael took both her hands in his own, leaning close. "Such eyes. How did they fit such enormous eyes into your beautiful face? They had to boil your skull to make it flexible to expand the sockets for those beautiful eyes."

He was trying to embarrass her, I guessed. She didn't blink. "Thank you, such a compliment."

Davidia wore her hair short and almost natural, but not all the way, not tightly kinked, rather relaxed into close curls. She was of medium height, more graceful than voluptuous. She had a face I'd call the West African type, a wide face, sexy, cute, with a broad nose, full lips, soft chin, a child's big eyes, and she looked out from deep behind them with something other than a child's openness.

Michael took over and ordered for us all, a little of everything, more than anybody could have eaten. Two youthful waiters both wanted the honor of serving us—serving Davidia—competing for it with a kind of stifled viciousness. Davidia seemed to accept this as her right.

As striking as she was, she had an unformed, girlish quality, and I was surprised to learn she'd interrupted her pursuit of a PhD to put in time at the Institute for Policy Studies, and more surprised to learn she'd interrupted all of that for Michael Adriko. I counted back, and this was the fourth fiancée he'd introduced me to. He didn't ask them to marry him. He asked them to get engaged.

Michael and I both talked a lot during dinner—competing to show off, I suppose, like our waiters. Michael volunteered nonfacts from his store of misinformation. "Nair has family in South Carolina."

"Georgia," I said. "Atlanta, Georgia."

"Family?"

"Everybody but me and my father."

"His father is Swiss."

"Danish," I said. "I'm half Danish."

Michael was about to speak, but Davidia said, "Quiet, Michael," and then, "I don't think I've ever met anybody from Denmark."

"Denmark is misunderstood. I'm not sure I understand it myself."

"I don't know what that means," she said.

"How did you and Michael meet—may I ask?"

"We met at Fort Carson."

"Were you in the military?"

"No."

"Good."

Michael said, "When I met Nair here in 2001, he was with NATO."

"NATO? Here? This isn't exactly the North Atlantic."

"NATO had people here two weeks after nine-eleven," I said.

"Are you still with them? What do you do now?"

I handed her a business card from my wallet. "Budget and fiscal."

"Who's 'Technology Partnerships'?"

"We crunch numbers for corporate entities interested in partnering on large projects with the public sector. In the EU, that is. We're not quite global. It's dull stuff. But I get around quite a bit."

Michael said, "When we met, Nair was with NIIA."

She waited until I said, "NATO Intelligence Interoperability Architecture."

"A spook!"

"Nobody says spook anymore."

"I just did."

"In any case, I wasn't one. I sent cables in plain English. Just comparing the project to the schedule, so they could revise the schedule to fit the project and go home winners every weekend."

"And what was the project?"

"Boring stuff."

"Nair had something to do with laying fiber-optic cable for the CIA."

"NATO doesn't deal with the CIA," I said.

"It was American stuff you were putting in the ground, don't try to fool me."

"All I did was wander around Sierra Leone like an idiot."

"And after that," Michael said, "Afghanistan."

"I was an idiot there as well."

"I can vouch for that," he told Davidia. "That's where I found him after a year's separation, in Jalalabad, driving a stolen UN car."

"You people!" she said.

"What a baby I was. I thought I was Colonel Stoddart or somebody."

"Stoddart?"

Michael said, "He got beheaded in Afghanistan."

"In the nineteenth century," I said, to dispel her shock.

"Oh, Stoddart—yes—"

"Thirty-five years old. Almost like me!" Michael said.

"To be clear," I said, "Michael was driving the stolen car."

"All the UN did was cower in their compound in Kabul, and get drunk, and watch people steal their equipment."

"Were you doing fiber-optic cable there too?"

"No."

"Nobody realizes this," Michael said, "but the US military has its own internet. They have their own self-contained system of cables all over the world. And communications bunkers everywhere."

"Bunkers? Like bomb shelters?"

"Technology Safe Houses," I said. "The ones in West Africa are probably rotting in the earth. Nobody cares about this place."

Davidia was drinking wine, which I wouldn't have recommended, but she'd chosen something Italian, and she seemed to like it. Every time she took a sip, Michael and I stopped talking and watched.

"Michael," she said, "you've never explained what you were doing in Afghanistan."

"Michael was my bodyguard."

He took offense. "I had many duties there. I transported a lot of prisoners."

"What about now, today," I said, "our duties now? Somebody please tell me. Are we here for a wedding?"

Davidia said, "Yes."

"So, Michael, this trip has nothing to do with business."

"Well, while we're traveling—we've always got our noses open for the smell of business."

Davidia laughed, and I said, "That came out wrong. But I get the message."

Michael said, "Davidia will be married wearing shoes of pure gold. And she'll keep them the rest of her life."

"All this meets with your approval?"

Davidia only said, "Yes."

"Are we really going to Uganda?"

Michael said, "We'll fly to Entebbe next week, is that all right? Can you come? Because in Uganda, they really know how to put on a wedding. I wish it could be a double wedding."

"You want two wives?"

"Be serious! Two brides and two grooms. I told Davidia you're engaged."

"On the brink of engagement," I said.

"Aren't we all!" Davidia said. "What does she do?"

"She's an attorney, but she works for NATO in Amsterdam—for your lot, actually. For the Americans."

"Nair met her in Kabul," Michael said.

"He's actually correct about that. But Tina and I weren't involved over there—just acquainted. She was a prosecutor for the UN, and Michael and I both knew her a bit."

"A bit? She wasn't one of Michael's, was she?"

"You think everybody's my girlfriend. Do you think I have unlimited time for sex?"

"That's exactly what I think."

"Before the UN," I said, "she served as a prosecutor in Detroit. Once she took part in a drugs raid and carried a machine gun."

"So she's dangerous. Is she beautiful?"

"Yes, but she's a little too smart for that. She keeps herself a bit plain. I prefer it."

Davidia said to Michael, "You'd parade me around nude, if you could."

"Nude except for sexy platform shoes. You've got it, so flaunt it."

"Sometimes," she said, "you have a thirsty face like a little boy." She laughed. She was tipsy by now. I hoped she'd do something stupid, something to break the beautiful image. She caught me looking. "You don't sound the least bit like Georgia. How much time have you spent there?"

"Very little. My father raised me in Europe, mostly Switzerland. I don't think he had legal custody—I think I was kidnapped."

"Is he still alive?"

"Both mother and father are living."

"When do you see your American family?"

Just the kind of question I like to deflect. But I found I wanted her to know. "I've had no contact with my mother or her family since I was eight years old."

"But you, you—" She was flustered. "You see your dad, right?"

"We get together every so often. He lives in Amsterdam too."

Michael was staring at me. "These are things I never heard about."

Davidia told him, "Maybe that's because you talk more than you listen." She said it with affection. I thought I was done, but she kept at me—"What line is your father in?"

"He's a physician at a teaching hospital. More teacher than physician, in other words. I'm afraid he's a little crazy."

"And your mother?"

"As I've said—no contact. I choose to believe she's happy."

"Then I'll believe it too," she said.

Now a beggar dressed in rags came out of the dark and wrote swiftly on the floor with white chalk: MR. PHILO KRON / DR. OF ACROBATICS. He started doing cartwheels in place while holding a platter of raw rice, never spilling a grain. He repeated the trick, now holding a glass of water, also without spilling.

The staff, the patrons, everybody ignored him, but Davidia said, "Michael, give him something."

Michael only offered him a scowl and said, "Don't encourage these people."

Davidia smiled and met the acrobat's eyes, or one of his eyes—the other's socket was scarred and pinched shut—and this inspired him to talk, or to signal his thoughts by a series of squeaks, as he seemed to be missing, also, one of his vocal cords. "Sometimes it's feeling like the Prophet was just here," he told Davidia, kneeling before her, touching her hand, trembling with the intensity of his message, "the Prophet himself, on this spot, and he went around that corner of the building there, and see, there, the dust still stirred up by the motion of his garments." Satisfied with that, Dr. Kron took himself and his piece of chalk back into the night, and one of our waiters came quickly with a rag and wiped away his title and his name.

•

Later, as we hailed a car in front of the place, Davidia took my arm and said, "What does a prosecutor prosecute in Afghanistan?"

"You mean Tina? Everything. It was right after the invasion. For a little bit there, the UN was the only law. She specialized mainly in crimes against women."

"*Was* she one of Michael's?"

"Are you jealous?"

"Are you?"

"Listen, whoever his other women were—you're not like them."

"Thank you," she said, and kissed me briefly on the mouth.

Michael said, "Are we taking this fellow to bed with us?"

"I bet he wouldn't mind."

"Look what you did, Nair—you got her ready for me."

I saw them into a car and said good night and strolled home down the beach, drunk, under such a multitude of stars they gave me light to see. The small action of the waves made a rushing, muttering kind of rhythm. The moon hadn't risen yet. Occasionally a school of phosphorescent flying fish swarmed upward out of the darkness offshore.

The Papa lay about a kilometer along from the Bawarchi. I arrived still drunk and looking forward to several hours of dreamless rest, but no such luck.

The power was off, the lobby dim. The night man napped in a plush chair by the door. I got him going and he handed over my key and a handwritten message, folded in two:

> I missed you on Tuesday.—H

This meant I had a date for tomorrow afternoon, Thursday, to negotiate the sale of the contents of my Cruzer. I would meet my contact, Hamid, at the Bawarchi—only by coincidence, as we'd arranged these details weeks ago, in Amsterdam.

I took the stairs upward three at a stride, quite suddenly and miserably sober. I rigged my portable hammock on the balcony and lay out in the sea breeze, and came inside in the wee hours when it rained. I lit the candle and opened my laptop. No internet. Off-line I wrote to Tina—

> I'm having a bad night. I miss you and even at moments your old cat and her monstrous ugly sister the dog. I don't quite yet pine for your Mrs. Landlady—what's her name? Mrs. Rimple?—but I'll probably even reach that point too before it's over.
>
> Just tried a bite of a sandwich, and it was stale. It's only been out of the bag for two minutes. God-

damn this climate, nothing gets dry but the bread,
the miserable bloody

—and heard the whining in the tone and stabbed DELETE.

•

As soon as day came I checked out of the Papa Leone and moved over to the Scanlon, third floor, almost where I could stomp my shoes and rock Michael's ceiling in room 230 below. Not that I'd have roused him, even if he were home. I'd had the maximum of Michael Adriko lately. And I'd only been on the continent thirty-six hours.

I stood in my room wondering how much I should unpack, not knowing the length of our stay, and deciding I'd give it all an airing—

I jumped as my door was flung open. I hadn't turned the key in the lock.

The manager stood there. Short, stocky, Arab. He looked as shocked as I must have. "I'm searching for the cleaner," he said.

All I could think of to say was, "You mean the housekeeper?"

"Yes. That's right."

"She's not here."

He shut the door and left.

I changed my mind about unpacking everything, and got out fresh socks and underwear and kept the rest in my bag.

One of my heads said to the other, He meant to search your things, and the other head said, Don't get jumpy, people make mistakes, and the first one said, Either way, my friend, they've got you talking to yourself.

•

"Life is short," Michael always says, and there's fear in his face when he says it, because he understands it, he means it, this life ends soon.

Michael is a warrior, a knight. Higher-ups command him, and he pretends to obey. The rest of us live as squires and peasants.

—So my report might have said, my second, and final, report from Freetown. It might have said also:

For him the world consists of soft spots and hard spots and holes, it's all terrain, and he works it, pausing only to eat, drink, shit, piss, fuck, or treat his wounds.

Michael identifies himself as one of the Kakwa, the clan of Idi Amin Dada, and his story runs thus: After Amin's exile, when the reprisals began against the Kakwa, the boy Michael was taken to Kampala and educated by kind Christian missionaries . . . But missionaries don't take a child from the village and put him in a city school. More likely he was kidnapped by a criminal gang and survived on the streets as a harlot boy.

He claims that having finished his secondary schooling, which I believe he never started, he joined the Ugandan army, entered the school for officers, and before receiving his commission was assigned to a unique training camp along the Orange River in South Africa, where Israeli agents—from the Duvdevan Unit, he sometimes says, other times he says the Mossad—instructed him in terrorist tactics.

True or false, what does it matter? Michael's truth lives only in the myth. In the facts and the details, it dies.

And while you, my superiors, may think I've come to join him in Africa because you dispatched me here, you're mistaken. I've come back because I love the mess. Anarchy. Madness. Things falling apart. Michael only makes my excuse for returning.

And if he thinks I'd like an army and a harem, Michael mistakes me too. I don't want to live like a king—I just want to live. I can't make it happen by myself. I've got all the ingredients, but I need a wizard to stir the cauldron. I need Michael.

—So my report might have read.

As for the actual report, I banged it out quickly in the basement of Elvis Documents. The crisscross shadows of the lights' wire cages, the choking musk of the concrete walls, also the thought of Mohammed Kallon tiptoeing back and forth overhead, none of these things encouraged settling in for a lengthy chat. I wrote:

> I've established contact. Changing stations quite soon. Details to follow in 48–72 hours.

"No lunch today," I told Mohammed when I came up from his basement, only five minutes after I'd gone down.

He was already rising from his alleged chair, saying, "I've had my lunch. What about dinner this evening? I've got some news for you."

"Dinner? No. Just tell me."

"Very good then," he said with clear disappointment,

"I'm to explain something to you. Michael Adriko was attached to the US Special Forces in eastern Congo. There's a unit there, you know, chasing the Lord's Resistance Army."

"I've heard about it."

"Now he's absent without leave—that's what I mean when I call him a deserter."

"All right," I said.

And so I could have reported as well that by his secrecy, his coyness, Michael Adriko had thrown up a screen against most of my questions, in particular the first one I'd asked: If our aim was Congo, or Uganda, what on earth were we doing in Sierra Leone?

Here was the answer, from Mohammed Kallon. Michael had landed here on the run, probably settling for any destination that would admit him with a Ghanaian passport. Not a bad choice, Freetown. Anything can happen here. Traitors and deserters can evaporate before your eyes.

Mohammed said, "Let's meet at the Papa for dinner."

"Halfway through you'd be saying, 'Why take me to an expensive meal? Just give me the cash.'"

"Well, certainly—I could use a little cash."

I gave him a wad of leones half an inch thick but nearly worthless, and walked out into the noontime's unbelievable heat.

One half block from Elvis Documents a man with a generator and a satellite rented time on his computer, and I sat in a collapsible chair, under an umbrella, beside his scrapwood kiosk, and found a Reuters report online. Its closing paragraph:

> The LRA mission will belong to about 100 special operators, Pentagon sources said. They declined to say which unit will be assigned to the mission, but a media report in the Colorado Springs *Gazette* suggested that the 10th Special Forces Group, out of Fort Carson, Colorado, will be the one. This unit typically handles special operations in Europe and Africa.

Despite the heat I walked to the Scanlon. I was angry. Not with Michael, as I might have been, but with Mohammed, because it was simpler.

Along my way I stopped at the Ivory Castle Hotel to talk to the baffling, inscrutable West African men who pretended to manage the air service piloted by the drunken Russians. We had to resort to the Russians because no genuine airline would take us aboard without Ugandan visas, although Uganda would issue them to arrivals at Entebbe without any problem—so Michael had assured us. I asked about the fares and schedule. The managers seemed not to understand why I would even want to know. I presented them with the white European's suffering weary smile, the only alternative to murder. Ultimately they revealed to me the prices and the times. Michael, Davidia, and I would get out of here in less than forty-eight hours.

•

At three in the afternoon I once again entered the Bawarchi. The patronage was light, the place was quiet. At first I thought my contact hadn't come, and when I located him, seated at one of the smaller tables, nothing before him but a pair of sunglasses, I thought he must be someone else, because I'd only seen him in business suits. But he was Hamid, the one I'd talked to several times in Amsterdam.

He waved me over and I sat down with him. He gave the impression of being middle-aged and fond of comfort, in a loose white linen outfit with a tunic, more Arab than Euro, except for his eyes, which weren't brown, but a washed-out gray. He had his sleeve pulled back as he checked his Rolex Commander wristwatch. He wore six jeweled rings, three on either hand.

"Exactly on time."

He handed me his phony business card, and I handed him mine.

"Do you want something to eat?" he said. "A snack of some kind?"

"Nothing, thanks. Have you ordered?"

"Won't you join me for some tea?"

"If you haven't ordered—"

"Not yet."

"Good. Why don't we walk on the beach?"

"Nobody hears us. We can talk."

"I'm nervous indoors," I said.

"Come on, don't be silly. Just tell me what you've got."

"You know what I've got."

"I want to know what I'm buying."

"Let's walk. I don't like it in here." I wanted us out of the public eye, because I couldn't be sure of his reaction to a bit of news I had for him. "Do you mind?"

He sighed, and then he picked up his sunglasses.

I donned my own as well, and we passed from under the roof and into a hot, steady breeze while the sunshine crashed onto our heads. Through the soles of my sandals I felt the beach burning. In our sinister shades, the only figures in view, I suppose we looked like nothing so much as a couple of crooks plotting mischief.

When we got near the water's edge, he stopped. "Now, before we get a stroke or dehydration or something—what have you got?"

"Exactly what I told you I'd have. Maps of the US military fiber-optics cables throughout seven West African countries. Mali is one of them. Also I have a list of the GPS coordinates for twelve NIIA Technology Safe Houses." Including, I might have added, the safe house in the basement beneath Elvis Documents.

"You're definite about Mali."

"Mali. Yes. That's definite."

Mali was the current hot spot. With Mali I had him hooked. Talk about a thirsty face.

"Let me establish something with you," he said, "and please forgive me: Do you know what can happen to a party who sells false product?"

"I would expect to be assassinated."

"Your expectation is precise."

"I'm not worried. It's very good product."

"What about the transfer?"

"A push of the button. I have things stored away."

"We can do it all digitally?"

"Correct. You never have to touch the goods."

"Do you still stipulate cash payment?"

"Correct. Cash only."

"And the price is twenty thousand US."

"No," I said, "not twenty thousand. That's no longer correct."

This was the bit I didn't like.

He started a retort, but stifled it. He must have been counting ten. "I don't understand what you're saying."

"The price is no longer twenty thousand. For you, out of your own pockets, the cost will be nothing—because we go in as partners."

"Partners for what?"

"We'll be equal partners in the sale you're making. I'm providing the product, and you're providing the client."

He bunched his mouth in an ugly way and made a sharp noise with his tongue. "It's completely unacceptable." He raised his sunglasses. "What are you thinking? You know nothing about my business."

"I think I do. The Chinese are all over this continent, and they're paying ridiculous sums. If they're not the people you're selling to, you're an idiot."

He replaced his dark glasses over his eyes. "I don't like this conversation. You're too forceful. You use a personal tone."

"I'm being emphatic, but only for the purposes of business. It's nothing personal. I'm just saying the Chinese will pay plenty for something good. And this is good."

"It was agreed. Twenty thousand US. It was agreed."

"We're beyond that point now. We're talking about a partnership. This is excellent product with long-term potential. Very long-term. The loss of this material will never be detected."

He clicked his tongue again and turned his back and walked toward the restaurant, leaving me by the shore.

A dozen meters along he called out over his shoulder, "You're a liar!" After that he didn't look back.

My head roared. Switching the price had felt like a bold move in a sport without rules, but what was bold, and what was stupid?

I took a look at his card. CREATIVE PRODUCTIONS / Film Plus Internet / Hamid Faisel / Managing Director.

In Amsterdam he'd had a different last name but had still been Hamid. He'd been chatty, sociable, kind of fun. We'd gone to a film together, *Zero Dark Thirty*, in English, the Hollywood action movie about the killing of Osama Bin Laden. Afterward Hamid made jokes about the great martyr. "It wouldn't be so funny to my relatives in Lebanon," he said. "But why should I care? Because I'm not really Lebanese. My mother is French, my stepfather also. I was raised in Marseilles. I am French. France is a happy country. Lebanon has turned into shit."—As I say, chatty. Today, in Freetown, neither of us had any jokes to make.

I gave him time enough to get lost, if that's what he wanted, and then I went through the restaurant toward the cars out front. Hamid was sitting at a table near the entrance with a cup and a saucer before him. I headed for the front without looking at him.

"One moment, one moment. Come on." He waved me in and I sat down with him once again. He had a pen in his hand. "How can I believe anything you say, when you're a liar?"

"You'll have a small sample to work with, enough to understand that this represents an ongoing intelligence mother lode to anyone who taps into the cables."

"What have they got to detect such tapping?"

"Nothing remarkable, unless there's been an upgrade in the last ten years. And there hasn't been."

"Give me back my business card, please."

"If you say so."

"You might decide to get in touch." He licked the point of his pen and took the card for a minute and handed it back with an e-address written on its blank side. The domain was dot-UK. "Only if you want to honor the original agreement," he said.

"Sure."

"Don't use the twenty-five."

He meant the AES-25 encryption standard, known as the American Standard. "Of course not," I said.

"And rotate your proxy every fifteen words."

"Sure. I hope English is all right."

"English, French, Dutch. I don't care. But choose your words—no red flags."

I tore a page from my notepad and borrowed his pen. "Here's mine. Maybe we can exchange ideas and reach an understanding."

He stared down at my e-address, but he wasn't reading. I waited. "All right," he said. "Where's the harm? Think about your price and let me know later."

And then I felt smug and thought: Of course, he can't pass this up. Not when it includes Mali.

"Send me your sample," he said. "Maybe I'll consider, that's all I promise. But you can trust my promise, because let me tell you," he said, "I'm not a liar."

Ending it on such a note, I didn't offer to shake his hand. I went out to the beach again. The heat matched my blood, both were beating, simmering. I walked the shoreline toward other restaurants visible up ahead, where cars for hire congregated.

I took off my sandals and wet my feet in the shallows, and I watched the ocean swell and shrink and listened to it sigh.

Here the sea is warm, like a bath. It's dark, not so blue, more like black, a lustrous black.

You wade out into it until you can't. You swim out farther until you can't. Then it takes you.

•

At a table outside the Quonset hut from which the drunken Russian pilots administered their charter airline—with its fleet of one, a commuter jet—we dealt with a young Leonean man who spoke faultless English, and as he held Michael's passport, I tried to sneak a look at it. Davidia was peeking too—at mine as well as Michael's. "It's US," I told her. "I have a Danish one too, but I never use it." Davidia's was American.

Davidia wore her safari garb, while Michael was dressed in a wrinkled suit and gray snakeskin boots. His outfit looked at first pink, but closer it was white linen with thin red stripes.

When Michael got his passport back, he let me have a look at it—a wilted Ghanaian document. "I told you I saved the Ghanaian president."

"A couple of times. At a minimum." I gave it back to him. "It's got less than two months left on it, Michael."

"Never fear. I've got family in Uganda, and just as many

in Congo. One of those places will claim me. I'll make the necessary inquiries."

We weren't at the Freetown airport, but at an airstrip well east of the city and next to the ocean. Our aircraft waited in a field of tall grass. I said to our young man, "That's a Bombardier Challenger, isn't it? The Royal Danish Air Force uses them for cargo."

"Not this kind," he said. "This is the 600, discontinued from 1982."

Davidia shaded her eyes with a hand and squinted. "Are you saying that plane is thirty years old?"

"The one you're looking at is a couple of years older," he said. "But it's a very good aircraft, so long as you don't overload it."

Michael said, "Nair—remember the Russian airline? The Freetown–Monrovia run during the war? Something Airlines?—something Russian?"

"It wasn't an airline. It was a renegade charter, just like this one."

"They were the only ones bold enough to fly to Monrovia."

"You mean crazy enough. Eventually they crashed, didn't they?"

"That's right, but not on the Monrovia run. That time the plane was coming from a secret rendezvous, loaded with processed uranium."

The clerk disagreed. "That's unsubstantiated, and in fact quite false."

"Were you there at the crash site?" Michael said. "If you were there, you were five years old."

"Processed uranium?" Davidia said. "You mean enriched?"

"Exactly right. The plane was overloaded with HEU stolen from Tenex."

"HEU?" Davidia said. "What's HEU? Who's Tenex?"—and as she seemed to be talking to me, I shook my head, and she said, "Where did it go down?"

"That's the beautiful part," Michael said.

"It's never been found," the clerk said. "But factually, it only had some inconsequential cargo aboard."

"U-235? Do you call that inconsequential?" But Michael couldn't expect to be heeded. He looked like a species of gangster in his pinstripe suit.

I tried a guess: "Highly Enriched Uranium."

"Nothing like that aboard," the clerk said. By his expression, he seemed to have taken a special dislike to Michael.

The runway was visible once you walked on it, packed red dirt hidden under tufts of beach grass.

The aircraft would be booked to capacity—otherwise the Russians would postpone, and that's why the weekly charter never flew weekly. With a couple of dozen other passengers, African, Indian, Arab, a few white Euros, we waited beside the terminal, a rusty ship's cargo container open at one end, nothing in it but a row of four theater seats. Nobody would have sat inside—the heat it gave off was startling. Clouds blanketed the sky, but it was bright, and the sea reflected it so viciously you couldn't look at the water.

A white Honda Prelude arrived at the Quonset hut and stopped, and nobody got out. I recognized the backseat passenger. I said to Michael, "Look there. It's Bruno Horst."

"Bruno, at our point of departure. Well—nothing funny about that!"

"I can't make out the man riding shotgun, but I don't doubt it's Mohammed Kallon."

I waved. Only the driver waved back. I recognized him too. It was Emil, who'd carried me to the Papa Leone my first day in Freetown.

Everything I'd touched, they were touching.

The clerk called our flight. As the others gathered their things I wandered over to the shore with my phone in my hand and, when the water stopped me, I opened the device and pried loose the SIM card and flicked it into the waves. If NATO Intel had a trace on it, let them trace.

On second thought, I didn't want the device, either. I made a wish and tossed it as far as I could out into the sea. I wished for magic armor, and the power to disappear.

I rejoined our group. As we boarded, a young fellow in an olive uniform ran a wand around each passenger's outline, fondling us in the places where it squeaked—that is, the men. He didn't touch the women. We climbed onto the craft up metal treads salvaged from old passenger busses and welded into a crooked stairway. Ahead of us a frail person, an African so ill as to seem genderless and colorless and weightless, was being carried up the steps like a bolt of cloth on the shoulders of two young men. "Going home to die," Michael said.

I sat against the window overlooking a wing and one of the two jet engines. Michael and Davidia took the seats one row behind and across the aisle. After the engines started, one of the crew—I assumed there were two—a blond man wearing denims, white T-shirt, and flip-flops, came out of the cockpit and wandered down the aisle, saying, "Is English okay? Okay, let's try it. I want to warn you of the safety features of this aircraft. Has everybody got the seat belt buckled? It's your choice, I'm not your mother. Okay," he said, "it's a trip of sixteen and one-half hours, stopping once at Kotoka International in Accra and once more at Yaoundé, and the final stop will be Entebbe. You'd better have a visa for Ghana or else for Cameroon if you think that's where you're going. If you need to get a visa for Uganda, it's all right, they can fix it at the airport without a big problem. Wherever is your destination, I think you can expect the customs to be serious. They're always serious with our passengers. They're too serious." He waved goodbye and re-entered the cockpit and closed and locked the door, leaving behind him an atmosphere of vodka.

I'd spent five days in Freetown and learned nothing—except that I could have landed in Uganda to begin with.

The craft took off over the sea, made a tight, nauseating turn, and came in so low it bent the grasses in the field beneath. We had a close-up view of the highway heading north, and one last snapshot of Freetown: an accident on the road—a farmer talking with both hands, a twitching bloody goat at his feet, a car with all four doors open, a sign stuck inside its rear window—SPLENDID DRIVING SCHOOL.

TWO

We got our Ugandan visas at the Entebbe airport without any trouble. Hungover from the long, rocking flight, with the two stops in between, at both of which they kept us suffocating in our seats for upward of two hours while the cabin's temperature rose to match that of the surrounding tropical darkness, I, for one, wasn't sure I was still alive, felt I might have entered some intermediary realm on the way to oblivion, and the smoothness of our passage among the Entebbe officials and through the terminal and out to the hired cars only mixed me up all the more. I thought we should go back inside and double-check these visa stamps. Michael said, "My people don't like senseless trouble. It's not West Africa. Relax." He got us into a car, where Davidia fell asleep instantly, her head on his shoulder, and we sailed toward our beds. Cool air reached our faces through the driver's open window—cool. From Lake Victoria, I gathered.

Thanks to Michael's budgetary strictures we stayed at the Executive Suites, a place with resale-shop paintings hung crookedly, but in all sincerity, on some of its walls, a "bed-and-breakfast," as Michael called it, a good two kilometers from the lake and from the real hotels. On a tour of its single story, looking for a bed that wasn't broken, I counted fourteen rooms. We arrived a bit too late for the breakfast.

I spent much of the day wandering muddy lanes in search of a phone and soon got one, another Nokia. I took a late lunch at a table in front of a quick-shop calling itself Belief Enterprises and loaded the device with minutes and sent Michael a text: "Note new phone. Have lunch without me. I'm at a table eating chicken, while chickens wander around at my feet."

Later Michael woke me from a deep nap by slapping at my door crying, "Nair, dinner is mandatory."

For three seconds I was awake, felt ready for adventure, very nearly got my feet on the floor—woke again still later with no idea where I was.

I checked my new phone. Another hour gone. Hymns filled the air outside my window, some nearby congregation worshipping in song, and then the unintelligible reverberations of a sermon through loudspeakers. By the time the preaching was finished I'd taken a cold shower and located myself in Entebbe, and it was Sunday.

I found Michael and Davidia at a round white table in the patio restaurant embracing and cooing among the remains of their dinner, spaghetti, probably from a can. I wasn't hungry. The happy couple drank Nile beer from the bottle and I had an orange soda and Michael told us we'd traveled southeast from Freetown about five thousand kilometers and had landed five kilometers north of the equator and twenty kilometers south of Uganda's capital, Kampala, and three hundred kilometers east of the Mountains of the Moon and the headwaters of the Nile River; that the elevation was some twelve hundred meters, that we couldn't expect temperatures to get above 30 Celsius, and that we'd better set our watches ahead to 8:42 p.m., because we'd lost an hour heading east; and then in a clear, sweet tenor voice he sang most of "Ain't No Mountain High Enough" to his fiancée, accompanying Marvin Gaye and Tammi Terrell, whose voices issued from the bartender's boom box.

I went over and got the barman to switch it off and taught him to make a vodka martini and drank one or two of them pretty rapidly.

When I rejoined my comrades with another drink in my hand Michael said, "I was just explaining to Davidia—we'll head north tomorrow for Newada Mountain. Or in that direction. North. Stanley explored there, looking for the source of the Nile."

"More will be revealed," I said. I was aware that lately I was drinking more than ever in my life. I couldn't relax or feel like myself in this region without banging myself on the head with something.

"My village is there," he told us, "in sight of Newada Mountain." Next he said, "I'm being communicated with by a spirit. Something or someone is contacting me. No, I'm serious. The spirits of my ancestors, the spirits of my village."

"What village? I thought you were some sort of—what the hell are you, originally, Michael? Some sort of displaced Congolese."

"I am exactly that. A displaced Congolese. And now," he said, "I'm going to replace myself." He took hold of Davidia's arm as if to hand her to me in evidence. "She's along because I'm going to marry her. I want her to meet my parents."

"I thought your parents were dead."

"Not my real parents. My other parents. The whole village is one family. Everyone is my mother and father and brother and sister. If the feeling is right, we'll be married right then and there."

Davidia said, "Wait—if the feeling is right?"

"If you're welcome. And I'm sure you'll be welcomed. The bride is always welcome, unless she comes from a clan devoted to stealing."

"And I'll be your best man," I said.

"The equivalent."

"Nobody's going to cook me and eat me, I hope."

"People don't quite understand," Michael said, and he may have been serious, "to be eaten pays a compliment to your power."

A couple of whores came in and sat at another table.

The boom box was back in operation. I talked Michael and Davidia into trying the barman's martinis. They had a couple each, and danced with one another. Between numbers we listened to the song of a frog who sounded like a duck, an insistent duck.

"I knew it from the start," I said. "Congo. I knew it."

"Not Congo, no, not necessarily."

Davidia said, "Isn't it time you told us where we're going? Where are your people located?"

"During the reprisals they were dispersed. We were uprooted and scattered. But they've reconvened. Relocated."

"Where, exactly?"

"Where? Quite near to Arua, in the northwest corner of this country."

"Uganda."

"This country where we're having our supper. Uganda."

"Not Congo," I said.

"Not Congo."

"And how do we get there?"

"We're taking the bus from Kampala."

"Come on! We'll take a plane," I said.

"It has to be the bus. You can easily see why."

"Why?" Davidia said.

He meant Horst, and Mohammed Kallon. If for some reason Interpol was on us, they could check the flight manifests out of Entebbe. I saw the logic. I disliked the conclusion.

"You'll get to view the countryside," he said to Davidia.

"Good! The bus!" she said.

"Arua is the birthplace," Michael informed us, "of Idi Amin Dada. In the month of March they celebrate his birthday."

"What? You mean the whole town?"

"Just a handful of people. But nobody stops them."

The bus . . . Out of pity for us all, I didn't laugh. "So we simply climb aboard," I said, "and go away."

"Yes. Day after tomorrow. Can you just come with me?"

"Sure. I'm drunk enough."

"Good. Stay drunk."

"What about you," I asked Davidia—"are you drunk enough?"

"I'm in love enough."

She had a somber glow about her, a smoldering vitality that warmed the air. She made me hungry. I wanted to smell her breath.

And the nightclub girls, one of them wearing a curly blonde wig, like a chocolate-covered Marilyn Monroe . . . The bartender didn't talk to them and they ordered nothing, they only watched me, and waited.

Michael's tongue was tangled in martinis—"I don't want to be a thumb," he said, "in the turd in the punchbowl of life."

"What?"

Michael was drunk. That meant he was in pain. He gripped a pen, he was writing something on a napkin. He tapped me on the shoulder and handed it to me. In the pleasant darkness, I couldn't make out the letters.

I told him, "I wouldn't have expected you to marry black."

Michael shook his head as if to clear it. Davidia stared at me. "What did you say?"

Right. What had I said? "The drinks are clobbering me. It's the altitude."

"You should have put food in your stomach," Michael said.

Davidia said, "Explain your remark."

"You mean defend it."

"Fine. Defend it."

"I'll explain it," I said.

"We're waiting."

"He's always had a weakness for the Middle Eastern type, that's all. The Persian princess sort of female. I apologize for talking out of turn. I do apologize."

She laughed. She was angry. "Don't twist yourself in knots."

It was only for Michael's sake I was trying to smooth things, but Michael wasn't even listening. "Back to another subject," he said. "I never answered your question about the Tenex corporation."

"Tenex?"

"Do you remember? At the Freetown airfield. We were talking about uranium. Tenex handles U-235 material from dismantled Soviet warheads. Dilutes it to ten percent pure and barters it to the United States."

"Jesus, Michael—again, the U-235?"

I've always thought it a laugh, Michael's obviousness when he means to be sneaky. No stage villain ever looked more the conspirator, leaning forward into his face's shadow, his head cocked toward the game, the trick, his right eyebrow going up, his lip curling in a sneer.

A quick, horrid intuition assaulted me.

Davidia placed her hand on my forearm and asked if I was okay. I said, "I'm fine, except I need to be smarter."

"Smarter isn't always better though, is it?"

"Good night."

I went over and made an arrangement with the whore in the blonde wig. She stood up, and hand in hand we journeyed to my bed.

She was drunk, also in some way drugged, and she passed out when we were done—perhaps before we were done, and I simply didn't notice.

•

Later I woke as the woman was leaving, and I locked the door behind her and lay in bed watching the Chinese cable station, a piece about fourteen baby pandas in the Shanghai zoo. A sudden rainstorm hit the roof like an avalanche and killed the city's power and sent all of existence back where it came from. I thought of the woman wandering around out there in the roaring dark.

On my nightstand I found the napkin Michael had written on. By the light of my cell phone I made out the words, but not their meaning:

He's my panda
from Uganda
he's my teddy bear
they say things about him
but I don't care
Idi Amin
I'm your fan!

—I read it several times. The rhyme scheme interested me.

•

Not long after six in the morning I heard, through the papery walls, the buzz of Michael's clippers and the shower running next door, and soon I heard someone going out. A few minutes later came a light tapping. I was heating water for instant coffee—the Suites provided a drip brewer but nothing to brew in it, only a jar of Nescafé. The tapping came again, and I realized it must be Davidia.

I got close to the wall and said, "I'm awake."

Her voice came quite clearly. "Come and see me."

"Should we meet in the restaurant?"

"Let's talk in here," she said. "Come over. Or around."

"I could easily come right through." Talking through the wall like this, I felt how close our faces were.

The lights in the hallway flickered on and off. The door stood open. In the random illumination she waited in a yellow silk robe, barefoot. She stepped aside and I entered bearing my cup and my jar of Nescafé.

"Where's Michael?"

"Taking his morning run."

The air tasted damp from the shower. Her underwear was lying around. I smelled her perfume. But she said, "It stinks in here. Sorry. Sometimes he sits down and smokes half a dozen cigarettes one after another. Doesn't say a word. Lost in his head."

She picked up a cigarette from the nightstand and put the end in her mouth. Looked around. Perhaps for a lighter.

"Do you smoke?"

She threw it in the pile of butts in the ashtray and said, "I'm so stupid."

"Let's have some coffee. Do you have bottled water?" She gave me a liter jug and I set about heating water in the brewer.

She sat on the bed. "We had a fight."

"I'm surprised to hear that. I mean to say—you were pretty quiet about it. I had no idea."

"He wanted to be quiet. So he could hear you through the wall."

"Hear me?"

"You and the girl," she said.

"We were quiet too," I said.

"We're a stealthy bunch of idiots," she said. "And I mean idiots." She got up but didn't know where to go. "I've been wanting to see you alone."

"Why?"

She paused. "I don't have a ready answer."

"Did you have something you wanted to say?" Seeing I wasn't helping, I added, "I'm only trying to help you figure it out."

"I wanted to see what we were like together."

"Oh." I devoted myself to the cups and spoons and Nescafé. "What were you fighting about?"

"I thought Kampala was the destination. Now we're going on to Arua."

"But last night at dinner you were ready to swing with it."

" 'Swing with it'? Who are you, Jack Kerouac? You reach way back into the last century for your Americanisms."

"Nevertheless."

"Sure, last night I was a real swinger. Alcohol affects me too. I didn't realize he wasn't telling us anything."

"Michael doesn't draw up plans. He weaves tales. Just let him be mysterious. If there was any way of hurrying him along, believe me, I would have found it by now."

"This is why I had to talk to you—to compare notes.

Can I trust you? No—I can't, can I?—I mean, trust you to be straight with me. What are we doing? I mean, specifically, you two—what are you up to? There's something going on, and he won't tell me what."

"There's nothing going on in the sense of—going on. We're traveling together."

"Why do you tag along?"

"I'm one half of the entourage."

"He assumes you're devoted to him. I'm not so sure."

"He assumes I'm devoted to getting rich. You know—exploiting the riches of this continent."

"And is that really you? A cheap adventurer?"

"Why do you call it cheap? Adventure is glorious. I don't understand why people put it down."

"I can't believe you just went off with that poor woman, in her silly-looking wig. Did you think to use protection?"

"This is a little crazy. Don't you think it's none of your business?"

"No. But don't you think I have reason to be crazy?"

"Drink this coffee," I said.

"Something's wrong with him, Nair. In the middle of the night he gets these sort of, I don't know what, nightmares, sleepwalking, talking in his sleep—really, I don't know what."

"Actual sleepwalking? Walking around in his sleep?"

"No, but—talking, thrashing—talking to me, but talking crazy, looking right at me, but he looks blind when I shine a light on him."

"Night terrors. Right? Violent memories."

"It's driving me nuts. It's scary."

"Tell me something: When did you arrive in Africa?"

"Tomorrow will make it two weeks."

"Just short of two weeks. Right on schedule for a melt-down. Nothing serious. A tiny low-grade implosion, let's say, of your American personality."

"I've traveled before. Don't condescend to me. I'm crazy about a man who's driving me crazy because I'm crazy about him. He won't tell me anything. He took my cell phone."

"Really? Jesus."

"He won't let me call home."

"Your people must be frantic."

"There's only my dad, and we don't correspond much anyway. He's bitter at me since I started doing work at the Institute. Still, I mean, if I could call him—I would. If Michael would let me. Why won't he let me? Is he always like this? Because it seems like something new."

"It's nothing new."

"You've seen it before. Paranoid suspicions. Taking away people's cell phones."

"I've been analyzing Michael Adriko for a dozen years. First of all—you realize he's a war orphan. He was born into chaos, and he's pathologically insecure. He keeps a stranglehold on the flow of information because then it feels like his life can't get away from him. But whatever you absolutely need to know, he tells you. Even though sometimes I'd like to torture him with electricity."

"Don't joke. He's been tortured before." It was true.

Davidia stood there holding her cup with two hands looking alone, and pitiable, and stupidly I said, "Are you really going to marry him?"

"That's what I'm here for."

"Do you really love him?"

She said, "Do you know who my father is?"

An unexpected query. "I guess not."

"Michael didn't tell you? My dad's his CO—the garrison commander at Fort Carson. Colonel Marcus St. Claire."

"Oh my lord," I said, "oh my lord." I jumped up to say something else and only said, "Oh my lord."

"Until I met Michael, I'd only known two loves: love for my father, and love for my country. Now I love Michael too."

"But you said your dad and you were on the outs."

"It's complicated. It's family. I'd say we're estranged. All the same, he loves Michael as much as I do. Everybody loves Michael. Don't you love him, Nair?"

"I can't resist him. Let's put it that way." And I added, "Oh my lord."

•

I went to the lobby, more on the order of a vestibule, and ordered some coffee. Soon Michael came through the doors in a powder-blue sweat suit and put his hands on his knees and bowed like that, breathing heavily, showing the top of his big muscular shaved head. Then he stood and whipped off his sweatband and wrung it out over the floor.

I waved to him. "Come here, will you?"

He came over.

"Sit down."

He sat down beside me on the divan, his leg against mine.

"Michael. You're pissing me off."

"Never!"

"Tell me once and for all, in full detail. What's this all about?"

"Do you like Davidia?"

"I don't want her here."

"What-what!"

"Not if you're up to what I think you're up to. And if it's what I think, then you're fucking up, man. You're fucking up."

He stared down at the palms of his hands for a bit and then showed me his face: a soul without friends. "Let's walk around. I'm still cooling off." But first he went to the counter and called for the clerk and begged a cigarette and stuck it behind his ear.

I followed him out the doors and into the wash of red mud that passed for a street. The brief stretch of morning had already baked it hard. At this elevation the air was cool enough, but the equatorial sunshine burned on my back. It was crazy to walk.

Michael strolled beside me gripping my arm with one monster hand and with the other massaging my neck, my collarbones. His face shone with joy and sweat. "It's good to speak honestly to you, Nair! Now it's time, now I can do that. Now I'm happy. I was desolate, but now I'm happy. Ask me anything."

"Jesus, Michael, where do we start? How about your military status?"

"I belong to nobody's military. I was an attaché merely."

"There's a US Special Forces unit hunting around eastern Congo. Looking for the Lord's Resistance. Were you attached to them?"

"That's correct."

"Did you run off?"

"That's an ugly rumor."

"Did you run off?"

"I didn't run off. I moved away in support of my plan. My beautiful plan—and yes, yes, yes, we're going to get rich, how many times do I have to tell you? Be patient. Soon you're going to see something. With one stone, I'm killing a whole flock of birds."

"Cutting through the muck—your status is AWOL."

"Detached. Detached is more precise."

"Next question. Are we messing around with fissionable materials?"

"Hang on, my brother."

Over the last few days his speech had lost its American flavor, and his stride, I noticed, had an African man's swivel now, and his shoulders rolled as he walked, like an African's. The lane climbed steeply here. He stopped to get a light from a vendor and then he was many paces ahead, on a rise, jogging toward the crest while puffing on his cigarette. I caught up with him and he said, "My brother, do you think our wedding ceremony involves U-235?"—with a false and sickly grin. What an amateur. When it came to fountains of falsehood—a bold artist. But a simple denial, one word, a flat lie? No talent for that.

"Hold on," I said, "let me catch my breath."

A shirtless beggar in khaki shorts approached, smiling and dragging one leg and crying, "Sahibs!" The leg was enormous from elephantiasis, as if another whole man clung to him.

Michael yoked the man's throat with one hand, in the

web of his thumb and finger, and lifted him so his horny yellow toes dangled a few inches off the ground and said, "Nothing today. Ha ha!" and set him back down. We walked on. To me he said, "I jog at six every morning. Do you want to get in shape with me?"

"No. I want you to tell me about U-235."

"Not yet. What else? Ask me anything, Nair."

A bit more, not a lot, had been revealed. No sense driving further against this foam-rubber wall. "How about this one: You're marrying the camp commander's daughter?"

"The garrison commander. Yes."

"This is too wonderful. Where's the unit from the Tenth?"

"Close by Darba, Congo."

"If we go up there—won't he want her back?"

"Whether we go or not, he'll want her back."

"He won't get a bunch of vigilante Green Berets on our tails, will he?"

Michael was silent in a way I didn't like.

"Will he? I'm not up for risking any bloodshed. 'Any' means not one drop."

"No, no bloodshed. They won't suspect we're anywhere near them."

"Let's just not go."

"Not go?" He turned in a complete circle, seeking a witness to my folly. "He says 'Not go'! Do I have to make it clear? Then I'll make it clear. Let me make it clear about my clan. It's as if I left a man for dead and ran away to save myself. Then the next day he walks into my camp covered with blood, ready to go on living. Can you imagine the shame you would feel looking in his eyes? That's the shame that makes me go back to my village. Can I make you understand? I'm going to marry Davidia. She'll be my life's mate. We've got to launch our lives together properly, with the blessing of my people. How can I make you *understand*? This is essential, it's not a gesture, it's not a nice idea—it's the essence of the thing. Without it, I'm nothing, and she's nothing, and we're nothing."

As he expressed these ideas he followed them with his eyes, watching them gallop away to the place where they made sense.

"And we're going somewhere called Newada Mountain?"

"Near there. I haven't yet learned the exact location."

"And yet you're sure your people have reconvened."

"I just know they had to come back together. It's the natural thing to do."

"It's essential."

"Yes. Essential. You say it like an empty word, but the word is full. It's the truth. It's about the essence of things. Nair, I can guess where you got your information about me. From Horst, or Mohammed Kallon. Fuck them. Officially I've deserted, but in truth I'm returning to the loyalty I ran away from. What is desertion? Desertion is a coin. You turn it over, and it's loyalty."

I agreed. "My, my. You've been thinking."

"A soldier must never think. In fact, when you're forbidden to think, it comes as a relief. Why did my mind start thinking?" His face was swollen with misery. "Nair, you're the most important friend I've ever had."

•

At five the next morning Michael had us traveling in a hired car through the darkness toward Kampala. As we approached the capital the traffic got thicker, and the air itself, with the smoke of breakfast fires and diesel fumes, and we raced under the attempted streetlights, many of them burning, turning the smoke yellow. Somewhere around here we'd get on a bus that would take us to the country's northeast corner. We hunted up and down unnamed streets until the driver gave up and put us out, and then the three of us stumbled over gutters and potholes among the hordes of street denizens waking up to the long slow overclouded African dawn, begging for assistance—we begging; not them. Michael got us to the booking office of the Gaagaa line, as it was called, a five-by-five-meter space completely covered with people asleep, who didn't mind being stepped on by others making for the clerk's cage. The clerk showed us a seating chart, and I wrote my name where I wanted to sit, up front near the driver, and Michael put himself and Davidia across the aisle.

As we boarded the craft I looked up and realized it must have been dawn for half an hour, but the sky was so cloudy no real sunshine made it through. It was good having a cushion to sit on, even a gashed and moldy one, but I couldn't understand Michael's cheery attitude, his eagerness amid this fleet of debauched luxury liners exported from Malaysia or Singapore in freighter-size lots of wreckage, throttled and punched into taking a few more gasps, filing onto the roads with their busted television sets and torn-off seat belts, full of Michaels. We stowed our gear in racks overhead and Michael made sure Davidia and I each had a bottle of water and a box of Good Life butter biscuits. From some sort of church in the building behind us, on the second floor, above the public toilets, came a chorus of singing.

Davidia arranged her long African skirt and pillowed her head on a folded scarf against the window and fell asleep. The passengers settled in all around, pulling their cell phones to their heads and talking. They smelled of liquor and urine and armpit. Michael now placed himself among them, resuming the mantle of African poverty—the way a civilized African does, relaxing the shoulders and calming the hands and letting down the veil over his heart.

The bus's woman conductor stood in the aisle and addressed us, giving us her name and town and then bowing her head to pray out loud for one full minute in the hope this journey wouldn't kill us all. She invited everyone to turn to the next passenger and wish him or her the same thing, and we did, fare ye well, may this journey not be your last, although one of these journeys, surely, will send us—or whatever parts of us can be collected afterward—to the grave.

Our captain was a small man in a crisp white shirt and gray trousers, with a beard and turban. He sat down and started the engine and rattled the gearbox, and in just a few minutes the speedometer, I had a clear view of it, topped 100 kilometers per hour.

Somewhere behind us in Kampala, somewhere in Entebbe, I could have found Wi-Fi, I could have sent an encrypted summary-of-activities to NIIA . . . Goddamn, such an SOA might have begun, you perfect assholes. You sent me into this mess but told me nothing relevant. Fully half of what I've learned, you already knew. You didn't mention any U-235, did you, though I'm willing to bet you'd heard rumors, and that's why I'm on this thing in the first place. And I'm not the only one on it, as I'm sure you're also aware.

You said nothing about Interpol's interest, and as for Michael Adriko's desertion, I had to hear about that from Mohammed Kallon, a cheap Leonean grasser. Are you after information? I might inform you that Michael Adriko travels incommunicado with his bewildered fiancée, who happens to be the daughter of the camp commander for the US Tenth Special Forces Group, and that yesterday I saw her brassiere lying around and it was white, imprinted with tiny pink flowers, but you probably know all about that too. In any case, if there's something I know and you don't, anything at all—you can wait for it at the bottom of Hell . . .

Three hours along the route, the highway changed from two lanes down to one. The rate of speed stayed at 100. Smaller vehicles drove off the road as ours sailed toward them. The big lorries, the twelve-wheelers coming at us with their manifestos painted on their faces—AK-47 MONSTER—FIRE BASE ONE—GOD IS ABLE—LIVE FOR NOW—gave us half the road's width, and on our left side our own wheels traveled into the muck. None of these maneuvers required any reduction of speed on the part of anyone.

We slowed down only for the accidents, getting on the margin to steer around a small wreck, later another, and then we met a big one that stopped traffic both ways. I'd been nodding off and opened my eyes on a smashed lorry, a smashed pickup truck, a car upended and torn down the middle and sprouting limbs and dripping with blood. Pedestrians peered into the shattered windows without too much discussion or excitement. It must have just happened—ours was the first vehicle to come along, nothing to block the view. A baboon crouched on the bank of the roadway watching. A second observed from fifty meters on. Neither acknowledged the other. I noticed a bicycle bent in two tossed down on the grass. Michael clicked his tongue. "They just won't slow down."

While we waited for some force of civilization to take charge of the catastrophe, people descended from our bus to stretch their legs, eat their snacks, laugh, talk, relieve themselves. The three of us joined them at the roadside. Davidia shaded her eyes with a hand and studied the baboons studying us.

Michael said to Davidia, "He's talking to you," pointing to an old man who approached us. "He is a magician." He looked less than magic, instead looked tiny and silly, sucking on a long purple sugarcane. "He says we are all captives of this world. We were stolen while we were asleep and we were carried here, and now we're held captive in this world of dreams, where we believe we're awake." While Michael translated, the magician laughed and hacked at his stalk of cane with his two or three teeth, snorting. He smiled brightly at someone he recognized across the road and turned away from us as we vanished from his mind. Michael said, "Someone just has to drag that pickup truck to the side, and we'll pass through." He went back into the bus. In twenty minutes the driver sounded his horn. People began climbing aboard. Michael told me, "It's not as bad as West Africa. But it's still a hard land."

All were aboard but one. In the field beside us Davidia, herself, was peeing—she gave everyone a big smile as she rose from her squat and dropped her hem and hitched her waistband with a very African, very female shimmy of her hips. I felt I was seeing her for the first time.

•

In Arua we took rooms at the White Nile Palace Hotel. Here was the palace, but we'd crossed the Nile twenty kilometers ago. We arrived at night and formed no impression of the surrounding neighborhood except by its sounds—goats and cattle, arguments and celebrations. Surveying the parking area and later the tables in the café, I judged we'd come among missionaries and relief workers—Médecins Sans Frontières sorts of people with good, big SUVs and clean hiking shoes. The grounds were well-kept and our quarters were comfortable. I hadn't quite expected that.

At dinner Michael was nowhere in evidence. Davidia and I shared a table with an elderly, exhausted French woman of Arab descent who told us she studied torture. "And once upon a time before this, I spent years on a study of the Atlantic slave trade. Angola. Now it's an analysis of the practices of torture under Idi Amin. Slavery. Torture. Don't call me morbid. Is it morbid to study a disease? That's how we find the cure for it. What is the cause of man's inhumanity to man? Desensitization. The numbness of the perpetrator. Whether an activity produces pleasure, pain, discomfort, guilt, joy, triumph—before too long the soul grows tired and stops feeling. It doesn't take long. Not too long at all, and then man becomes the devil, he laughs at his former scruples, he enslaves and tortures without compunction." The woman's taut, quivering neck, her mouth opening and closing . . . Halfway through her dessert of ice cream with chocolate sauce, without a word, she got up and left the table.

"Is she coming back?"

"No. She's paying her bill," I said.

"She seemed possessed."

"You attract a certain type, don't you? Orphans and magicians and circus people. You draw them to you. I don't know how."

"I'm interested, and they feel it."

"Where's Michael? I haven't seen him since we checked in."

"As soon as we dropped our bags on the floor, he went out."

"Where?"

"I don't know. 'Seeking word.' That's all he said."

"More will be revealed."

•

But not revealed immediately. Whatever Michael was working on, it kept him away a lot the next two days. When it wasn't raining Davidia read airport novels by the pool, in a tropical two-piece with a wraparound skirt, while I sat in the thatched shade with my laptop open on the bar, looking busy. The pool was kidney-shaped. Why? Why shaped like a human organ? Frequent downpours kept it brimming over. People rarely swam in it. An arm's length above its surface, pairs of mating dragonflies whipped to and fro. Once in a while Davidia unwrapped herself down to her bikini and dipped herself in the water.

For restaurant and poolside music, American country tunes with a dash of rockabilly, the same forty-five-minute tape played all day long.

I wrote to Tina:

> Well, no internet this AM at the White Nile Palace (Palace for Whites) Hotel. Writing off-line at the moment. No Wi-Fi here. We have to queue up for internet at the manager's office.

A light rain began. Davidia left the area with a wave. She had very high, very round breasts. She wore sandals whose red color against her brown feet looked somehow violent. I reached beside me for my coffee and knocked it from the bar, and it shattered all over the tiles. I'd put myself on a seventy-two-hour moratorium—no spirits, no wine, no beer. A somber young waiter with a push mop came to look after the mess.

> In its relationship with Emmanuel, the manager, the office computer is sort of a cartoon villain, coming up with some new way to thwart him every time he approaches it—this time it was a warning beep that wouldn't stop—and his procedure is to start whacking whatever parts look whackable and twisting wires like they've been bad little wires and taking hold of the monitor with both hands and shaking the shit out of it, and today he gave the wall plug a good hard kick—not so stupid, really, because you do often get new results around here by wiggling the wall plug. Or snapping it with your finger. The people who work under him all know how to handle the computer just fine, and if the network's up, they can make it happen, but Emmanuel, he just starts

> right in on the contraption like he's carrying out an old vendetta, and I've learned not to ask him to try, except for entertainment.

I tried and deleted several ways of getting onto the next topic, and finally wrote—

> Have you heard anything from Grant or that Major Kenworth guy, or any of those other boys in Sec 4?

—Section 4, Internal Inquiries, counterintelligence, the spy catchers. They hunt the traitor.

> Let me know if anybody comes over from there just to say hi. I'll tell you what it's all about later on, when we're together again.

—and deleted the final sentence and wrote instead, "I've put in for an opening over there, to tell the truth," and deleted *to tell the truth*, "and if I have a shot at it, if they're interested in me, they'll probably do a little snooping."

•

I woke and dressed fast without showering, ridden by a desire, an absolute lust, to get it all done this very moment, plus a feeling I wouldn't get it done at all. I skipped breakfast and flagged one of the motorbikes waiting outside the hotel, and we traveled as fast as the engine could propel us toward the Catholic radio installation. Gripping my laptop with one hand and my life with the other, I made up my mind not to ride one of these things again. The night's rain had slicked the road going into town, and quick maneuvers around potholes or out of the way of death sent us gliding in zigzags over the red mud. Bursts of adrenaline drained me and calmed me. The forward charge slowed down as we mounted a long steep hill toward three large towers in a compound of low buildings, the Catholic communications center.

At the gate a uniformed guard searched me, and a laminated security pass went around my neck. The guard walked me over to the nearest of several adobe buildings, and there a kind woman in a nun's habit led me to a large room and sat me down before one of three computers at a long counter against the wall. She took a chair by the door. For the moment, it was just the two of us. I logged on with a password and immediately logged off.

While I waited, I heard the roar of a soccer game drifting up from the school at the bottom of the hill.

Pretty soon a blue-uniformed Ugandan soldier entered the room. I sensed him coming but stared at the screen until he touched my shoulder and said, "Please come," and led me to the Secure Communications Environment, the "SC lounge," or the "SC café." It looked like the room we'd just left. Only one computer console here.

This place had nothing to do with NATO, except in the way of "courteous exchange," as it's called in the business. The safe communications here were an operation of the British, MI4 or 5 or 6 . . . May I reveal a fact? I don't know how many MIs there are. In any case, it was nothing to do with NIIA. As far as I'd been allowed to know, NATO maintained no safe sites anywhere in Uganda for communications. The Americans like to say "commo"—I think it's silly. Using my own laptop, I checked my list of e-mails. One from NIIA. I didn't open it.

Another one, from Tina: a photo taken in a mirror, her face hidden behind the camera and her breasts exposed. Not a word of text.

I sent her what I'd composed off-line, and added:

> Nothing has happened since I wrote the above. I've spent my time listening to the BBC on a little radio or watching the images of Al Jazeera on the satellite TV, when the TV works. Emmanuel has permanently bested the hotel's computer and it just sits there half dead. Nobody can use it now. It's not a communication device anymore, it's capable of making a few high-pitched noises understood only by itself. Therefore I just took a half hour's trip across town to the Catholic radio station compound, where they have a media center with three computers & Wi-Fi.
>
> Don't forget to let me know if you hear from Sec 4.

—and felt I was hitting the thing too hard and deleted the last line and wrote:

> I thank you from the bottom of my scrotum for the glimpse of your beauties. I hope I can assume they're yours.

Nothing from Hamid. I'd expected nothing. It was my turn to talk.

I switched to my own keyboard. As he'd suggested, I

didn't use the American Standard. For a lark I used PGP, and in accordance with Hamid's wishes I rotated my proxy after every fifteen words:

> 230K dollars US.
> 50-50 split.
> Currently in transit.
> Will return to site of previous meeting when we have a deal.
> Suggest date exactly 30 days following previous meeting.
> Sample product: Basement Elvis Documents Freetown.
> NIIA safe site. Check and see.
> Don't answer until the answer's yes.

Having suggested a date, I heard the clock start ticking. Today was October eleventh—I'd have nineteen days to wrap things up with Michael and find my way back to Freetown. An easy schedule. But Africa wipes its mess with schedules.

I opened the communiqué from my boss:

> Let's not overlook opportunities for filing. Check in daily. I don't add "when possible." Check in daily.
>
> No amount of detail is too great. Err on the side of inclusiveness. Give us an abundance to sift through and ponder each day. Every day. Daily.
>
> From this point forward, consider that a mission imperative.

I replied:

Nothing to report.

—and closed the window.

•

The rain came hard. The dining room's fine vaulted ceiling apparently leaked profusely, and when Michael and Davidia and I entered that evening looking for dinner, the maître d' came at us with a push mop, driving a minor flood before him out the doors. On a hoarding on the step, a list of the cocktails on special—"Safe Sex in the Forest," mostly vodka, and one called "The Pussycat," whose main ingredient was identified as Baboon Whiskey. Time to lift the drinks moratorium? My thirty-dollar Timex watch said not even close.

The musical fare had changed—today, fifties pop, specifically "Smile" as rendered by Nat "King" Cole. Nothing else. Just "Smile." Over and over. "Smile" . . . "Smile" . . . "Smile" . . .

Michael had turned up two hours before, dangling a set of car keys. "Toyota Land Cruiser. Four-wheel drive. Full of petrol."

At dinner Davidia wanted to know when we'd go riding. "Soon. It's all ours."

I wasn't so sure. "Where did you get it?"

"From Pyramid Environments."

"Pyramid? Who's that?"

"Pyramid Environments. Security. I know all those

guys. The manager's office is in Arua. I know him from Fort Bragg."

"Bragg? I thought you were at Fort Carson."

"And Bragg—I told you that. At Bragg I trained Colombian commandos. The US assists them in going after the drugs racket down there. Everything was done through translators. Let me tell you something you already know . . . working in simultaneous translation is exhausting. It's like walking everywhere on your hands, and never your feet."

"So you've told me many times," Davidia said.

"I don't like the situation over there," Michael said, meaning the situation at another table. "These guys don't look right. They're up to something."

"Doctors Without Borders."

"Then why don't they go someplace and play doctor? First we see them at lunch, and now at dinner."

"Good lord. Is it possible we're following them?"

"Perhaps we should be."

Davidia glanced at me as if to say Help.

"Nobody's spying on you," I told Michael.

"Wait a minute. That one is Spaulding. Remember Spaulding?"

"I remember. That's not Spaulding."

Michael got up and went over to them.

"I hope he's not about to be rude," Davidia said.

"He's just being Michael."

"He's getting pretty crazy, Nair."

"You know what? I think he's right. It's Spaulding."

"Who's Spaulding?"

Spaulding possessed a great mop of platinum hair. I wouldn't have guessed such a thing, and I hadn't recognized him. As it happened, I'd never before seen the top of his head.

Michael brought him over. Spaulding didn't sit down. Pretty soon Michael would tell us he'd been the one to give Spaulding his very first sight of death. He'd told me this story many times.

"Here's Spaulding." To Davidia: "Spaulding is MI6."

Spaulding didn't mind. "He introduces everybody as some kind of spy."

"Have you chucked your turban?" I asked Spaulding.

"A turban's all right in Afghanistan, in the winter."

"So you were never actually some kind of Sikh?"

"Just keeping my head warm," Spaulding said.

"What's your religion, then?" Michael said.

"Lapsed Catholic."

"I myself," Michael said, "am a lapsed animist. This is Davidia, my wife-to-be."

"Congratulations, then, the two of you."

"Davidia—Spaulding is with MI6."

"I don't hang out with MI6," Spaulding said, smiling. "They're all homosexuals."

Michael said, "I showed Spaulding his first dead body. In Mogadishu."

Spaulding said, "It was more like two hundred dead bodies. All laid out neatly side by side in the street. Fresh-cooked."

"Remember the dust devils? Two kilometers high. That's where the legends of genies come from."

"You couldn't have been more than thirteen or fourteen. Your voice hadn't changed."

Michael produced a soprano: "Ayeeeeee!—My voice will never change," he went on in his man's baritone.

"I didn't meet Spaulding till Afghanistan," I said.

Spaulding studied me. "Really. Have we actually met?"

"Here comes our food," Michael announced. "None for Spaulding."

"Have a lovely evening," Spaulding said, mainly to Davidia, and rejoined his table.

Davidia said, "Jesus Christ. You people!"

I looked at Michael—looking back at me. "And there you have it," he said. "It's already time to leave town."

•

The White Nile Palace Hotel had proved in one respect far too proper for my taste, but that afternoon, as I sat at a table near the bar trying to make sense of the hamburger I'd just been served, a little brown slut with a wig of short red hair came in and stood within reach of my arms and started wrapping and unwrapping the skirt that covered her bathing suit as she queried the bartender, ignoring me and inflaming me, and I thought, Thank goodness, at last, a reasonable woman. I got her to sit down with me and asked her name. It was Lucy. She was friendly enough. I felt us on the brink of striking an arrangement.

The PA played "Jingle Bell Rock." Two American-sounding women swam up and down the pool with gentle strokes, side by side, conversing about the Bible and God and spiritual challenges.

Michael Adriko turned up at the pool's far end. He wore black bathing trunks. I supposed he could swim, but I'd never seen him at it.

He was talking to a Euro, a white man. It was rare to see Michael looking serious, rare to see him listening intently. I wished I could read the man's lips. He was of middling height and middling all around, mid-thirties, with thinning, colorless hair. Rimless spectacles, a short-sleeved dress shirt tucked into dark corduroys and come untucked at the back—a civil servant sort, he seemed to me, except that he wore the shirt half unbuttoned to display a thick gold necklace.

I moved to the bar and tried to catch Michael's eye, wondering if I should be introduced. I didn't catch his eye. I wasn't introduced.

I took up my cell phone and asked Lucy to excuse me, I had to make some calls. She said, "Maybe you need to call your boyfriend," and went to the bar to pout and say nasty things about me.

The two men each sat on the edge of a recliner, heads bent toward one another. I took a stroll around the pool pretty much in the manner of someone who had no idea what he was doing, passing behind them in order to—what? Smell what might be brewing—hostility? Conspiracy? Conspiracy, I thought.

I walked past them and out the back gate onto the grounds, and I took note again of the man's heavy necklace, which had tainted his neck's flesh with a greenish collar. I walked around a bit, then came back past the pool and through the bar, heading for the restaurant.

"Just give me a minute," I said to Lucy as I passed her. "I won't be two minutes."

I took a table in the restaurant and kept an eye on Michael and the other. Again the PA was playing "Smile" and had been playing it, I realized, for quite some time.

After one more full turn through the song, the man got

up and came toward me through the patio door, staring at me hard. He looked no more dangerous than a mathematics instructor, but my face flushed, I felt it—he passed me by and went out the front way. I watched out the window as he left the grounds by the gate, waving to the guard.

Michael was coming into the place.

"Join me for one second," I said.

He glanced around strangely, apologetically, and I realized that in his swimming shorts, he felt undressed.

I said, "Michael. What-what?" He sat down across from me and I said, "Who was that guy?"

"Well, he's a businessman."

"Are we in business with him?"

"Exactly."

"Do you want to tell me what it is?"

"Right. Things are in motion. It's time for full disclosure."

"Tell me."

"Come to my room in ten minutes."

I nearly exploded in his face. "If now is the time, why ten fucking minutes?"

"What's your hurry?"

"There's a girl I want to talk to."

"This is slightly more important."

"Why ten minutes?"

"Davidia's napping. I'll kick her out."

After he'd gone, I went back to the pool after Lucy—she was lying in the big rope hammock cuddling with a fat African fucker.

•

At the Palace the rooms occupied circular bungalows modeled after the local huts, but a great deal larger and roofed with rubber shakes, not straw; four rooms to a bungalow, each room a quarter circle, each with a verandah, a door, a bathroom, two windows side by side. This one had a bed, a desk, a TV, and a standing electric fan, just like mine. A couple of shelves and hangers on a rod—no closet.

I looked around for evidence of Davidia. The room had been cleaned, and everything was stowed, or hanging. It didn't look as if anybody could have been napping here.

"Full disclosure."

Michael unfurled a black shopping bag and dumped the contents on the bed: bright yellow electrician's tape wrapping a package the size of an American softball.

"Pick it up."

It was heavy for its size. "Feels like a couple of kilos."

He went hacking at the tape with a penknife and soon laid out before me a shiny lump of metal no larger than my thumb, on a rag of odd-looking material.

It looked like gold. I assumed it was gold. I prayed it was gold.

"What's this stuff it's wrapped in?"

"That's a bit cut from the smock you wear when you get an X-ray. It's lead-lined."

"Oh, shit," I said.

"That's right."

"Uranium."

"Very correct."

"U-235?"

"No. It's polished, but it's just ore. As long as it fools a

Geiger counter . . . Superficial authenticity, that's all we're looking for. It comes from southern Congo. The Shinkolobwe mine."

"Not from a crashed Russian cargo plane."

"No."

"You don't actually have a planeload of enriched uranium."

"I told you—full disclosure. There's nothing else. Have you heard of the Manhattan Project?"

"Sure."

"The uranium for that came from the same mine, there in Shinkolobwe."

"Looks as if a dog just squeezed it out its ass."

"A little lump can make a very big bang."

"If I touch it, will I get cancer?"

He laughed. I held it in my hand.

"I'm in the process of parlaying that bit of dog business into one million dollars US."

As if he'd opened a gash in me, all the tension ran out. I dragged the chair away from his desk and sat down. "So it's a scam."

"Of course it is. Do you think I'm running around with enriched uranium? If there was any U-235 on the market, New York City would be nothing but a crater already."

"And who's our friend, with the fake gold necklace?"

"Fake?"

"Didn't you see his neck? He's probably poisoning himself with gold spray-paint. I didn't like the way he came at me in the restaurant."

"He's calling himself Kruger, probably because he's South African. He saw you cruising around us. And Nair, it's genius.

The minute he saw you, I improvised something: you're the bad scientist."

"I'm the mad scientist?"

"The bad, the bad, the bad. You're the renegade engineer who recently examined the crash site for the Tenex corporation. You reported to Tenex there was nothing there. No uranium material. But you lied. It's there. You kept the truth to yourself, and you're selling the crash site's coordinates. Just a few numbers on a piece of paper. For one million cash US. It's too brilliant, Nair."

He paused for my reaction.

I couldn't see where to begin. A bit of rain started on the roof above and the leaves outside, and we listened to that for a while.

"You're the verification," he said. "We meet with Kruger and his partner, who's bringing a Geiger counter. We give them this shiny radioactive object as proof of possession, and you verify what I say about the crash site. Then on to the big swap. One million."

"But, Michael, have you thought this through? Or thought even a little? How would this scam work? Take me through it, step by step. What are the steps that lead to the moment when the money's out on the table?"

"By the time the money's on the table, we'll have a lot of guys to help us. After our meeting with Kruger and his partner, we'll have twenty-five K US as our payment for proof of possession. With some of that money, we'll get a squad together. Congo is full of brigands. M23, Lord's Resistance—plenty of warriors, and nothing to do all day."

"And then what? Cowboys and Indians? The money's on the table, and a bunch of guns come out?"

"I'll handle that part. You'll just handle the oily parts, because you're good at that. But the answer is yes. Armed robbery."

"You skipped over my real question. How do you get the money on the table?"

"When we meet with Kruger and his partner, we'll tell them that as soon as they have the big payment prepared, we'll be prepared to turn over another X kilos, say five kilos, and that's all we could carry from the crash site. We promise them the coordinates to the rest."

"And for telling them this fairy tale they'll give you twenty-five K?"

I heard him say, "Twenty-five," and then the rain outside came harder and washed out his words. I said, "What? What?"

"Twenty-five K immediately, Nair. In our pockets. Then we go from Arua to Congo and we find my villagers, my family. A beautiful wedding takes place. Then we make arrangements for the final contact and the rest of the payment. It's going to be a big payment, Nair, very big. Big."

"Right. One million. You already said."

"I haven't said it to them yet. Maybe I'll say two."

"Who's going to let you string them along all that way with just this little piece of dogshit?"

"The question to ask is—who could pass it up? Who could say no? If the claim is at all credible, they have to give it the full treatment."

"Credible? It sounds completely and obviously false, Michael—can't you see that? What words can I use? Nonsensical. Impossible. Out of keeping with reality."

"Reality is not a fact."

"Around here it certainly isn't. God."

"Reality is an impression, a belief. Any magician knows this." Like a cartoon villain, he rubbed his hands together. "Oh my goodness, Nair, you just tickle them in their terrorism bone, and they ejaculate all kinds of money. If you mention the name of one of the Muslim Most Wanted—boom, they put on a circus for you."

"You've skipped another question, haven't you?"

"What. What's the question?"

"Who is this 'they'? Are they a fantasy too?"

"Of course not. Kruger works for them."

"Who? Who are we dealing with besides this Kruger? Do you even know?"

"We're dealing with the Israelis."

If I'd had to stand up from my chair at that moment, I'd have failed. I was that shocked, and that much afraid. "Then you're dealing with the Mossad."

"Their involvement is likely." And he seemed proud of it. He smiled with all his teeth.

"You're scamming Mossad."

"They know me. If I say I have it, they've got to take me seriously and get together the cash."

The rain roared, or it was my head, but in any case the sense of things rushed away on a flood. "Michael . . . Michael . . ."

"Nair. Nair." He got his face close to mine as if he thought I couldn't hear. "I know those people. You *know* I know them. I was trained by them."

"Michael, be quiet."

"Let me tell you about it."

"No. I'm feeling bewildered. Please shut up."

He complied. I didn't say a word. In the silence, which was nevertheless quite loud, his folly bore down on us like a tremendous iceberg. Its inertia was irresistible. In this room, in Africa, reasonable arguments were just mumbo jumbo.

"Is that enough quiet? Can I talk now? Because I want to explain one thing: I've got contacts, I know Mossad—ever since my training in South Africa. I can call them anytime that we want to cancel, and the whole thing's canceled. Never happened."

"Well, Jesus Christ, man—call them now, and call it off. Cancel everything. Mossad? You're insane."

"All right. I'll cancel if you say so."

"I just said so."

"But let's wait until we take it one tiny step further along. Let's meet with these guys and their Geiger counter, and walk away with twenty-five K. Then no more. Nothing further than that."

"No brigands versus Mossad. No showdowns at the table."

"Exactly. And if they don't like our lump of shit tomorrow—no loss. At least we tried."

"Tomorrow?"

"Yes—tomorrow. I told you, full disclosure."

"Fuck it, Michael. I'm done."

I got up, making a loud noise with my chair, and headed out the door toward a place to be determined later.

"How done?" Michael called after me.

•

In two minutes I arrived at the bar pretty nicely drenched. I took a table where I could watch the storm.

At the bar sat Spaulding, his cranium wrapped in a big white turban. He pointed at it. "What do you think?"

What I think—I thought to myself—is you're spying on me.

I checked my watch. Time to lift the drinks moratorium. An hour past.

As I looked around for the barman, Spaulding came over to me. "Shit, Nair, I sort of didn't recognize you yesterday. You know—without the uniform." He set a full drink before me, saying, "Cheers, mate. It's made with Baboon Whiskey."

Like that, I drank half of it down. "Have a seat."

"I really can't. Car's waiting. I'm checking out."

I nearly said, Good. "Where are you off to?"

"Oh, God knows. The itinerary's a bit complicated. Entebbe to start. What about you?"

"Just here. Then home again."

"Home again to—"

"Amsterdam."

"Amsterdam! I love the hash. Do you go to the coffee shops?"

"Every day. Wrap up in my turban and get out my hookah and set fire to all manner of shit."

He laughed and said, "Happy trip, Nair," and headed off briskly, with a sort of half salute that knocked at his stupid head-wrap.

A bit sweet, but the drink had a kick. I signaled the barman. "Let's try a vodka martini."

Rain swept across the pool's face, and then it stopped. The sky was half-and-half—one storm had passed, another was coming. My first drinks in three days were going to my head, expanding my consciousness. I didn't like it. I gulped the vodka without tasting it and made my way to my bungalow and changed into shorts and a long-sleeved shirt and lay down. The TV lit up when I tried it. I watched Ugandan news, a report about a pair of twins conjoined at the shoulder—in other words, a two-headed baby—who had died, and then one about a child whose face had been eaten by a pig. Its fingers as well.

This information drove me out to a chair on the verandah. The sky was stuffed with thunderheads nearly black. I shut my eyes yet felt aware of the garden at my elbow, the blooms opening as if in a time-lapse, the stalks lengthening. Blossoms like dangling red bells, blossoms like tiny white fountains, fuzzy yellow caterpillars on brown twigs, a squad of snails lugging their small shelters up the spears of a plant.

The moment was dark as evening, but all was bathed in a great vividness. The rain shot out of the sky, hard as hail. A wondrous assurance lifted me, a force positively religious invited me to stand and shed my shirt, to drop my shorts and kick them from my feet. No need of clothes when clothed in African magic, and I walked naked across the grounds through the booming and the lightning with the sweet rain pouring all around, and soon I stood looking down into the swimming pool. Everybody else was indoors, and through this whole experience no other person was visible anywhere in the world except the bartender, all alone behind the bar under his awning a few yards from the poolside, watching as I jumped into the water and drowned.

From this dream I woke to another: I lay on my back beside the pool while Michael Adriko kissed me, breathed fire into my mouth and down my throat. I rolled over retching and coughing, my lungs tearing.

I came awake again on a lower rung of reality, still lying on my back, but now in my hotel room, wrapped in a shroud, shivering. Michael sat beside me on the bed.

I said, or tried to say, "You spat in my mouth."

"What happened to you, Nair?"

"Somebody drugged me."

"You didn't drug yourself?"

"I had one whiskey and one martini. Maybe the olive was bad."

"Bad? You mean evil?"

"What? Stop talking to me."

"Davidia is here," he said.

"Where?"

"Where? Here!"

"I'm not there," her voice said, "I'm here, on the verandah. Can you hear the crickets? Are those crickets?"

All around the music, like little bells. "Some sort of insect, yes," Michael said.

"Spaulding did this to me. Was it Spaulding, do you think?"

"It could be anything. A virus, a bite from a spider, or even a spell, a curse—people have such powers. I've seen too much to laugh at it."

"That fucking towel-head dosed my martini."

Michael laughed with such vigor that Davidia came in and looked at his face and said, "Are you all right?"

"You should have seen Fred's expression!" He meant the bartender. "Like the aliens were landing in his pool!

Seriously," he said, "he must have dragged you from the pool himself. He was wet to the waist. His shoes are ruined."

"I'll give him some money," I said.

The rain had stopped, and Davidia was correct—the creatures had resumed, the bugs that chimed like porcelain, frogs that belched like drunkards, and now more frogs, snorting like pigs. A suffocating sleep fell over my face. I came under its shadow convinced that Spaulding had poisoned me.

•

The next morning I asked for Spaulding, and Emmanuel, the manager, said he'd settled his account and left in a taxi for Arua's small airfield. Flying where? No commercial planes this morning, according to Emmanuel. Only the UN plane to Yei, in South Sudan.

I continued on to the restaurant for my appointment with Michael Adriko. I'd promised to meet him there and tell him my decision.

There he was, near the blaring television, doing nothing, not even watching it. "Well?"

"I haven't decided."

"Take your time. Up to ten more minutes. Don't sit down. Walk with me," he said, already moving, "I've got to see about the gas."

"Is it a long drive?"

"Just into town, over by the market, but you know the rule—half a tank is empty. You remember the rule."

I remembered.

When we came to the parking lot, he paused. "As of right now, the process is halted. You see how easy it is?"

"I get uncomfortable when you stop in the middle of walking to make a point."

"At any moment in the procedure, we can say 'enough.'"

"I understood the point."

"Then understand this one: Do you really want to go back to that boring existence?"

"Never."

This much was true, the only true thing between us.

By now we'd reached his borrowed Land Cruiser. We both got in. The engine caught quickly, first try.

The guard held the gate wide open for us.

It was a years-old model, much like the blue-and-white Land Cruisers we'd often borrowed from the UN in Jalalabad, sometimes Kabul. Too much like. It even smelled the same inside, like spilt gas and dirty clothes.

"Are you ready?"

"No. For this? No."

•

We stopped at a filling station where a woman topped off our tank, and we waited.

"Near the market, you said?"

"That's all I know. They'll call me with the meeting place. What time is it?—eleven-thirty-three," he informed himself. "They'll call me in the next half hour." We sat side by side on the vehicle's rear bumper, Michael studiously smoking, blowing white puffs upward through the brown fumes and the red dust, under the yellow Shell insignia. After the call, he pocketed his phone and threw down his cigarette and stomped it like an insect. "We're off."

We left the SUV in front of a place called Gracious

Good Hotel, under care of the taxi drivers loitering there. Michael, a bright red zippered daypack slung over his arm, guided me across the street toward the market by way of a narrow alley with light at the far end, its crevices roiling with crippled beggars—many were blind, and as for the others, they seemed to look through your own eyes and down your throat. Ahead of me Michael was a bent silhouette, handing over a crumpled bill. "My name is Michael," I heard him say, "pray for me." An old woman caught the money between her leprous paws and turned her sightless eyes up toward him and her lips moved below the noseless hole in her face, praying, "Michael, Michael," not for him, but rather to him, to the deity Michael . . . And crash, back into the daylight—it never happened . . .

I caught up with Michael at a clothier's stall. He was looking at a coat of fake black leather too hot for this region. He set his mirrors on his scalp, gripped the sleeve, touched the fabric with one finger. I didn't know if he was trying to buy something or just delaying, looking out for a tail.

The latter. When we left the market square he led the way into a dry goods store across the street. Inside we made our way directly down the center aisle to the back of the store, where a woman napped in a collapsible chair, and we asked her for another entrance. She pointed through a curtain, we passed through it and out into a side lane, then up to the left—and I recognized the street, and saw our Land Cruiser parked just a block away.

He handed me his daypack. "Take charge of the little morsel."

"Of course." Lethargy and nausea overtook me. It felt like it weighed fifty pounds.

Michael said, "I go first. Wait until you see me come out again, then you'll come and join me. It may take a few minutes."

"What's going to happen in there?"

"Before I bring you on the stage, I'll say I want to see the cash. They'll say no, but this way I get to review the environment."

"And then what?"

"It's two South African guys—Kruger is one, you saw him. You'll verify everything I tell them, right? Then I'll go with them. You can stay there—it's that café there, you see it? I'll go with them, we'll sit in their car or something with the sample and their equipment, and we'll make the exchange. And I'll come back in and collect you, and then back to Nile Palace."

"Where's their equipment, do you know?"

"Ah—you're thinking smart now. If it's not in their car or somewhere we can walk, I'll make them go get it. I'm not driving off with them."

On this sunny street, where earth-moving machines worked over piles of red dirt, improving the surface, and generators clattered in front of the shops and schoolchildren in green-and-white uniforms walked home for lunch, all this sounded reasonable.

"Stop breathing so fast," Michael said.

"I'm fucking nervous."

"Good. It helps you look the part. Just don't faint." He left me standing there and in order to keep my mind off itself I studied the nearby billboard exhorting the use of condoms and followed the progress of a small car over the ruts and small boulders from one end of the block to the other, its horn playing the first six notes of the "Happy Birthday" song. Looking around for something else, I spied Michael already back outside, standing in his own spotlight in his aviator sun shades as if in support of the warning stenciled beside him: DO NOT URINE ON THIS WALL 30,000 FINE. And he wore the fake black leather duster from the market. I was nervous to the point that I hadn't even seen him make the purchase.

Michael must have sensed it. He took my arm and kept me going as we went inside. I was living one of my persistent nightmares: I step onto the stage, it's time to speak, I don't know my lines. In this particular bad dream the stage was a four-by-four-meter dirt space enclosed in ironwork and roofed with tin, with a sign on the left saying SIMBA DISCO / PHONE CHARGE ACCUMULATOR AVAILABLE and on the right a Bell Lager clock with one hand, counting only the minutes, and wooden tables and benches. We sat down across from the South Africans.

They were a half-and-half team, like Michael and me. The black one, I assumed, was Zulu, and could have been one of Kruger's math pupils, but he looked in his thirties too. He wore his sunglasses on the back of his shaved skull. In most other respects he seemed to be trying to resemble an American rapper: a hooded sweater, baggy hip-hop shorts I hadn't seen anyone wearing in Uganda. A word about this Zulu's shoes. They were purple joggers, elaborately designed and, by the look of them, enclosing enormous feet. There's no explaining why I should have been so penetratingly aware, at this moment, of anybody's fashion choices. Kruger suggested a drink, and I certainly concurred, and now came the moment when I discovered the East African quick-shot—a square plastic envelope that would fit in your palm and holding one hundred milliliters of, in this case, Rider Vodka—Sign of Success. You chew off a corner and slurp. I bought several, several. The floor was tiled with discarded packets.

Michael produced a cigarette and called for a light, and the barman brought over several for sale. Michael had to try three or four of them before he got one that worked.

Kruger said, "Everything here is fake."

Michael said, "Only my heart is real," and put away his cigarette.

I wasn't taking in much, only the Rider Vodka. Remarks were delivered, there was talk of a Geiger counter, the location of their car, mention was made, in fact, of roentgens, but of all this I registered one exchange only: Michael said, "Nice necklace, brother," and Kruger said, "I like yours too," and when Michael thanked him, Kruger added, "It looked good on my friend before you stole it," and Michael said, "Who? What friend?" at which point, as if time had skipped forward, the three of them were standing up and fighting. The Zulu had Michael from behind in a bear hug, or was trying to pin his elbows, while Michael twisted side to side and the Kruger fellow thrust with a knife at Michael's chest and belly, then at Michael's throat.

Another skip—the Zulu lay on his back, wide-eyed, struggling to take a breath. Michael had hurt him somehow. I had an impulse to act, an image flitted through me, I saw myself taking two steps, jumping onto the man's chest, standing on him, keeping him down. No part of me acted. I experienced it as a question only—shouldn't I, shall I. I didn't. Now the seconds passed more fluidly, as if a stuck film had caught in its sprockets, and I watched the movie, which wasn't like the movies after all, not even like a boxing match on TV. I heard the initial thumps, then my hearing turned cottony, and I remember Michael's eyes—they watched, they looked, they moved here, there, they gauged—when he had his target, he locked on Kruger's face, not on his hands, though one hand gripped the knife in preparation for downward thrusts—

Michael danced backward, knocked a bench over between them, plucked at the table—a salt shaker in his hand; he threw it hard, it struck the man's chest, and Michael followed its arc, picking up the bench as he closed on his opponent, ramming the flat seat against him. Kruger fell backward as Michael's feet left the floor, one hand at Kruger's throat, the other still holding the bench in place, and his weight stuck the man to the table. His fingers closed on the carotid arteries, and Kruger lost conscious swiftly—a matter of a few seconds—managing to slash at Michael only once with the knife, which sailed to the floor, along with the bench, as Michael stood and snapped Kruger's arm over his knee. The breaking of the bone was quite pronounced. Deaf with adrenaline, I nevertheless heard that sound crisply. I heard it echo back into the room from the surrounding hills.

Michael wasted no time continuing the contest. He signaled me, I stood still, he came close, gripped my wrist, and before I formed even my first thought about what was happening, we were both in the Toyota and moving along as Michael steered with both hands, saying, "Wrap my arm, wrap my arm." His right forearm bled in spurts. He extended it across his chest toward me, steering with his left hand, and

I understood at last, and found my bandanna and wrapped it around a long gash that showed the yellowish bone. I tied it with a square knot. “That’s going to need stitches,” was his first remark since the action had begun. “So much for South Africa,” was his second.

•

Michael pointed out the White Nile Palace as we passed it. “I want you to drive back here after you drop me at the hospital.”

“Where’s the hospital?”

“I’ve seen the signpost up here a couple of kilometers. We go to the right. After that I don’t know.”

We rumbled across a wooden bridge. Ahead of us a pedestrian, an old man, jumped up on the railing to save himself.

“Well,” I said, “I wasn’t much use to you, was I?”

“But, Nair—what’s there, between your feet?”

“For goodness’ sake.” His red daypack.

“You grabbed my bag. You saved the most important thing. The valuables.”

A couple of minutes off the main road we found the hospital, a campus of one-story structures of concrete and brick, the Church of Uganda Kuluva Hospital, according to the sign at the guard post. The guard waved us down and peered through the window and waved us through when he saw the blood. “Nurse is coming,” he said. “Proceed to Minor Theatre.”

The door to the building called Minor Theatre was locked. Michael squatted on his haunches with his spine against the wall, smoking, while the blood seeped from his bandage and pooled between his feet. His eyes were bright and he gave off a certain energy.

He looked, I have to say, in better shape than I felt. I stood upright, but only to prove I was able. "I wish I'd made one tiny fucking move to help."

"I didn't need help. Did you hear his bone breaking?"

"God. I didn't even drive the car. I've always known I've got zero courage, but I don't like to be reminded."

"There's no such thing as courage. It's a question of training. You know, I'm not merely trained in unarmed combat—I'm the instructor."

"Maybe you should instruct me."

"I instruct you to stay by my side. You'll win more fights that way."

At the entrance to the grounds a car came to a sharp halt, and the man calling himself Kruger more or less fell out of the passenger door into the arms of his driver and the guard. The guard dragged the chair from his shack and sat Kruger down in it, and he and the driver—who was not the Zulu—carried Kruger in it toward another building with his shirt off and his arm bound up in it all bloody.

Michael waved with his own wounded arm. "No hard feelings, mate—next time I'll kill you."

Kruger sailed past in his chair with his eyes closed, chalk-faced and uncomprehending. His partner was nowhere around.

"I don't know what kind of mess we're in," I said.

"I think we're better off in Congo now."

"How did all this come about, Michael? Who were those characters?"

"I'm sure of this much: they weren't Mossad. Just a couple of jokers Mossad has on a string."

"In other words, Mossad has you marked for death."

"If Mossad wanted me dead, I'd be dead. Mossad works very tight. They use teams of six or seven or even more and they train and plan very carefully, and they get it done every time. They don't use idiots who attack you in a café. These guys were just associates, like me. But I believe them this far—I believe Mossad gave them money. That's why that fool pulled a knife. They wanted to keep my payment for themselves."

"This scam is over," I said, "finished, okay?"

"Agreed."

"Because it pisses me off when I go along with stupid ideas."

"You're pissed off now. I see that. Okay."

"I wish I had transcripts of the conversations that led to this," I said, "the conversations you had with those guys. I bet I could show you a dozen places where they were obviously—obviously—playing you."

"In the end, you have to go by instinct."

"You trust too Goddamn much."

"Is that really a fault?"

"What? *Yes.* A fatal one. The life you lead, the people you deal with—do you think it's just teddy bears hugging marshmallows?"

He laughed at me.

I wished Kruger would stab him again. "You trust the wrong people," I said. "Believe me."

•

This hospital had been established in 1848, according to the sign at the entrance, and originally as a place for lepers, according to Michael's nurse, who prepared the sutures and such on a tray. No doctor arrived. She stitched the wound herself. "We will close the laceration in two layers," she told Michael. "It's deep."

"How long do you think this will take?" I asked.

She was jabbing a swab down into the damaged area. "The sutures must go close together." I took this to indicate a lengthy procedure.

"If I had some water, maybe I'd clean up the car a bit."

"There's a stream there"—she pointed with her chin—"running behind the morgue."

"Where's the doctor?"

"The doctor is sick."

The guard abandoned his post and found me a bucket and led me to the creek behind the small brick mortuary, the stink of which came over the transom and into the afternoon, but nobody seemed to notice. I went back and forth with the bucket until I'd flooded the car's floorboards and turned the bright red mess into a faint pink mess, and then I went about peeping in windows. In a dirty concrete room behind a door labeled MATERNITY WARD, I saw Michael's assailant, the fool who'd pulled a knife, true name unknown, stretched naked on a bare mattress on a metal bed. He was alone in the room, the only occupant of a dozen such beds. The maternity ward's only patient. He had a round, simple face, and he breathed through his mouth. His arm lay out beside him, still bandaged with his shirt.

Michael's nurse, when I returned to them, was being

assisted by a young girl dressed in the green skirt and white blouse of the local schools. Work on the wound seemed to have ceased while Michael chatted with a police officer in a close-fitting uniform, all of it—even boots, belt, and helmet—crisply white. His large sun lenses gave him the face of an inquisitive insect.

"Officer Cadribo is making a report."

"Ah," I said. "Good."

"My friend Roland," he told us all, "will bring my fiancée. Did you see the route? It's just through the gate to the road, then turn left, then right at the main road."

"Hannington Road," said Officer Cadribo.

Michael told him, "We're staying at the White Nile Palace. We'll meet you there around suppertime, all right? The incident is hardly worth mentioning, but you have to make a report, we understand that. Let's make it an occasion. We'll buy you dinner." He wrapped my shoulder in his good hand and drew me close. "Go to the hotel, collect our things, and get Davidia. Check out and come back here."

Just to be talking, I said, "How's the wound?"

"We're waiting for just a few more cc's of Xylocaine," the nurse said.

Michael said, "We tried finishing without it, but God—it hurts! I can't hold my arm still."

Michael and the cop began talking Krio or the local one, Lugbara, faster and faster, laughing, their remarks ascending to the tenor register.

As I left them, Michael said, "Remember—you're driving on the left!"

•

Packing was nothing, three changes of clothes—and now one less, as my bloody jeans and T-shirt went in the trash. I called the desk and asked how to call a room and they said they'd patch me through.

Here, as in West Africa, land-line phones were answered by saying, "Hello?" and then taking the receiver away from the ear and staring at its silence before replacing it to the ear to listen a little more to the silence.

"I said it's Nair."

"Nair. I hear you. Where are you?"

"I'm in my room."

"Go ahead."

"Can you handle it if things get a bit more up-tempo?"

"What are you saying?"

"Well—just that we're breaking camp. Would you mind getting all your gear packed in the next few minutes? I'll help you carry everything to the jeep."

"What's going on? What's happened?"

"Michael's moved up the schedule a bit, that's all."

"Moved it *up. What* schedule?"

"We really should leave in the next few minutes."

"God. God. God. Is Michael there? Let me talk to him."

"He's tidying up some loose ends. I'll come round as soon as I'm packed."

"Nair, this is ridiculous. I'm not going anywhere."

"Then at least pack Michael's things for him, will you, please? I'm coming to your room. I'll see you in a few minutes."

When I knocked on the door, she said, "It's open," and I found her sitting sideways on the bed. She was dressed, except for shoes.

I saw no evidence of packing. "Do you mind if I shut the door?" She gave a little wave, and I shut us in and said, "The journey resumes."

"I don't think so."

"If we're going at all, we really should be pretty brisk about it."

"I'm not kidding. I've had it."

"All right. But I've got the Land Cruiser, and if we're going, now's the time."

"Where's Michael?"

"I left him in conference with some of his cronies. We'll stop and pick him up." She didn't move. "I'm your chauffeur." Not even her hands. "Sorry if the news is sort of sudden."

"So here's a piece of news," she said. "The lyrics for 'Smile' were written by two guys I've never heard of named Turner and Parsons."

It seemed to me they had two soft suitcases and two knapsacks. "What if we just shovel your worldly goods into your luggage?" I took some shirts off the rod. "Do you want the hangers? Let's leave the hangers."

"But the melody was written by Charlie Chaplin for his 1936 film *Modern Times*."

I stopped messing around. "How did you find this out?"

"I went online in the manager's office. It was driving me crazy. I thought maybe Irving Berlin—I was rooting for Irving Berlin, I don't know why. I guess I've always liked the name."

"I see. Did you get a chance to catch up on your e-mail, then?"

"No. Michael doesn't want me to. You know that."

"Have you been in communication with anyone?"

"No! I just said no!"

"Right. I just wondered."

"Is it any of your business?"

"That's just the thing, Davidia. Our business is getting all mixed up together now. Yours and mine. I hope you realize that. If you realize it, this is going to be a whole lot easier."

"What is? What's going to be easier?"

"Can I take a chair?"

"You're taking my things. Why shouldn't you take a chair?"

I sat down. "There's a lot you haven't been aware of. Nothing sudden is happening here. More is just suddenly being revealed." I took a moment to frame my thoughts. I don't know why. I'd imagined telling her this many times. "We talk about how the world has changed since the Twin Towers went down. I think you could easily say the part that's changed the most is the world of intelligence, security, and defense. The world powers are dumping their coffers into an expanded version of the old Great Game. The money's simply without limit, and plenty of it goes for snitching and spying. In that field, there's no recession."

"*That* field? *Your* field. It's obvious you don't work in some bank. It was obvious all along. You're CIA."

"Goddamn it. Ma'am, I am not in the Goddamn CIA. Don't lump me in with that lot."

She seemed about to speak, then didn't. I got up and sat beside her on the bed.

"You're sitting too close."

I moved closer. "But the truth of it is you're partly right. I don't work in a bank. I'm still with NATO intelligence. I'm here on assignment, actually, and the assignment is Michael Adriko."

"What? *Why?*"

"Michael's in trouble."

"Oh, Jesus. What's he done?"

"He may get out of it. You know Michael. But I think we'd better get out of it first. You and I."

"You and I?"

"I'm leaving on my own, and I think you'd better come with me."

"What for?"

"For whatever it's worth."

"For how long?"

"As long as it lasts."

"As long as what lasts?"

"Let me get you out of this."

"To where?"

"Back to Freetown. For a start."

"Why?"

"I've got business there. I can set us up."

"Nair, there's nothing between us."

"Come here. Let me hold you."

"Are you crazy? Stop touching me."

I had to stop, or I couldn't talk. The feel of her skin took my breath away. "I've known Michael for almost twelve years, and all this time I've thought I was infatuated with him, and I was wrong. All the time I've known him I've been infatuated with you. Waiting in infatuation for you to materialize. For him to produce you, conjure you, bring you, fetch you."

"Oh God," she said, "you're complicating this impossibly. You're making it impossible. Why do you have to be crazy too?" She stood up and started piling things on the bed. "What's Michael's plan? If any."

"He's going to Congo."

"And you're not."

"That depends on you."

"I think I'd better go."

"I think we'd better not. There's no law over there. The government has no writ. The cops, the army, psychotic warlords—they all take turns robbing anyone who's not armed."

"Then why don't you leave us now?"

"Because I can't. I couldn't bear it. Not without you."

"This is awful. Shut up."

"Once you've had a look at the place, you'll want to come with me."

"I'm going with Michael. Take me to Michael."

"I'll take you wherever you want."

"I've got to. I can't just disappear. I have to hang on till Michael's situation is . . . stabilized or something. Or at least clarified."

She put a bag on the bed and started filling it like a pit.

"Hold up for a bit. Will you? Okay?" She didn't. She kept packing. "Davidia. I didn't mean to scare you."

"Well, you did scare me. I'm scared—of you."

"I got crazy. I don't want to make you crazy too."

"Too late."

"Have I forced you into this decision? Because I didn't mean to put you in a corner. Wait a minute." She didn't pause. "Stop packing for a second."

"I'm going with Michael now, and I think you'd better take me to him."

"Are you sure? Are you sure?"

"Yes!"

"All right, fine. Just a minute. Look at me." She settled down. "I shouldn't have said what I said."

"I agree."

"I'm crazy."

"I said it first."

"So we agree on that too. So will you keep all this quiet?"

"Quiet?"

"Don't tell Michael."

"I've promised Michael I won't talk to anybody, now I promise you I won't talk to Michael—is that what you're saying?"

"Let me be the one to come clean with him, that's all."

"When?"

"Not right away."

"How long do I have to betray him, then?"

"Not long."

"How long exactly?"

"Two days exactly."

"Forty-eight hours."

"Correct."

"Promises to him, promises to you, and everything is secret from everybody else. This is what we call a situation." She seemed to see some humor in the thing.

•

To make ourselves more visible I lit the headlamps. Nobody else did such a thing, none of the bikes or vehicles set themselves apart.

Davidia said, “This is blood, isn't it? How badly is he hurt?”

“He needed quite a few stitches.”

“Where's the hospital?”

“Actually it's back that way.”

“Then why go this way?”

“Couple of errands.”

For these conditions I drove too fast. It was nearly 4:00 p.m. I had no idea how late the Catholic communications center might be open. Nevertheless I stopped at a vendor's shack and bought all his hundred-milliliter packets of spirits. Then I stopped at another vendor, and I did the same thing. Still I had less than a couple of liters. Before I left the hotel I should have gotten the biggest bottle of rum, or tequila, whichever had the bigger proof. Baboon Whiskey, if that's all they had. But I'd forgotten.

On the way up the long hill in the middle of Arua I nearly stopped again for another such transaction, but the sight of the towers at the top lured me on. “I'm stopping up here at a place with internet,” I told Davidia. She said nothing.

Across the road from the gates, I turned off the engine and said it again. “If you have someone you want to communicate with, here's the place to do it.”

“Just hurry up. I'm worried about Michael.”

“You can wait with the guard.”

“I'm fine right here.”

When I got out, I went around to her window. She didn't roll it down. “Will you be all right?”

“Will I?”

“If you get uncomfortable, lock the doors.”

I heard them locking even as I turned away.

•

I had two e-mails, the first from Hamid:

> Firm and final offer is cash funds 100K US for you.
> If your answer is yes, we meet same place same hour.
> Cash takes time.
> Your share 100K US. Final offer.

I liked his figure. I didn't like his next one:

> Will meet 4 weeks following date last meeting.
> Not 30 days. 4 weeks exactly. No fallback. One chance.

On the one hand, the money was set, and it was good money. But with his other hand he'd ripped two days from the calendar. I closed my eyes and set about composing a comeback, a counteroffer, and then scotched it. I had nothing to offer.

I opened the second e-mail: several hundred angry words from my boss at NIIA. Before I'd read half, I deleted it.

I banged at the keys: "Hello, you idiotic shits. Are you waiting for my report? You can wait till Hell serves holy water."

I pressed DELETE.

Again I banged on the keys, this time at some length:

> Goddamn you. You smiled sweetly while slipping a rocket up my ass and lighting the fuse. Now you want to dress me down?

Would you cunts please explain what British MI is doing at my hotel?

Would you cunts care to describe Mossad's involvement in—what shall we call it—this affair? Investigation? Cluster-fuck?

All of you, go fuck yourselves. Fuck each other.

I hold the rank of captain in the Army of Denmark. What has any of this got to do with Denmark? What has any of this got to do with me?

Why have you put me in a position to be murdered?

For three seconds, four seconds, five, my finger hovered over the DELETE key, and then I pressed SEND.

I logged out, plugged in my own keyboard, and went to PGP. I wrote back to Hamid:

Sold.

THREE

[OCT 15 11PM]

All right, Tina. The chief captor, the witch doctor, the general, the jailor or kidnapper or whatever he is, has just showed me my favorite thing in East Africa, a plastic baggie that would fit exactly in a shirt pocket, and shows me the label, "40% Volume Cane Spirits 100ml," before biting off the corner and sucking it dry, explaining, "It's for the cold," and tossing it aside, and I notice, right now, that the dirt floor of this big low hut we're in is littered with similar packets sucked empty and tossed aside—paved with them—"Rider Vodka" and "ZAP Vodka" and the Cane Spirits. I'm familiar with these packets, in fact many of these empties were mine-all-mine as recently as one hour ago, when they stole them, yet I don't perceive any gratitude in the black lacquer faces of these drunken soldiers all around us. What I do perceive is that this place smells powerfully of unwashed humans.

I just saw a single firefly flash upward. Or a capillary exploded in my brain. The truth is I'm a little drunk too. And this won't be one of those pitiful attempts to explain "how I got into this mess," because there's no sense calling it a mess until we see how it all turns out. Sometimes you just get stuck. That's Africa. Then you're on your way again without any idea what happened, and that's Africa too. And while you're stuck, if they give you a pen and paper?—you might as well.

As to why I have no computer, it isn't because they took mine away from me, but because as Michael and Davidia and I headed toward the Congo border in a Land Cruiser borrowed, now stolen, from Pyramid Environments, with our guide or abettor, a Congolese whose name I didn't catch, Michael stopped the car on a bridge over some tributary of the White Nile River and said, Here we'll toss our communications, and threw his phone out the window. Davidia chucked hers as well, and I was glad to get rid of everything (although my laptop and second keyboard were guaranteed GPS-untraceable, and my phone was already a replacement. I didn't want the weight of them anymore, that's all). It was sunset. Below us people washed their vehicles in muddy water up to the axles, the drivers splashing the red dirt off their rumpled pocked and sagging Subarus and such. Davidia said only one thing: "How long do you have the car for?"—"What?"—"When do you have to return this vehicle?"—"Oh—it's flexible," Michael said with a wide smile, as if describing his mouth, "it's quite flexible."

My friend and your friend Michael Adriko, that is, and his fiancée, Davidia St. Claire. You knew I went to Freetown on a hunt for Michael. I found him all right, with Davidia on his arm, and I'll catch you up on all the rest as time allows. To put it in shorthand, Michael's enthusiasms, let us say, had us leaving Uganda in a rush for DR Congo on Oct 13, just a couple of days ago. We'd jumped from Freetown to northwestern Uganda, a town called Arua, where I last heard from you by e-mail and where I last saw your breasts, and I wish I'd downloaded them . . . Earlier, at Kuluva Hospital in Arua, while getting his flesh stitched together after a fight it's pointless to explain, Michael had enlisted a guide to show us a hole in the border, because none of us had Congo papers. When Davidia and I got to the hospital, Michael introduced this man, a skinny little guy in bright blue trousers and a T-shirt that said, I Did WHAT Last Night? and told me to give him one hundred dollars.—When he's got us through to Congo, I said.—Fair enough, Michael said.

Daylight was almost gone as we got near the border, a good circumstance for people smuggling themselves, and we passed among groves of tall eucalyptus, Michael driving like an African, far too fast for the crumbling red-dirt surface, I mean fast, 90 or 95 KPH mostly, scaring the bikes to the side by means of constant beeping, using the horn much more than the brakes, oblivious to the children, goats, ducks, trucks coming at us, the overloaded busses appearing around road bends, leaning on two wheels, and women walking down the road balancing burdens on their heads, mostly basins full of "white ants"—centimeter-long termites they sell in the market as snacks. I've never tried them, but it's a comfort to realize that every couple hundred meters or so across this land, a chest-high berm teems with nutrient morsels. One of these women crossed our path, her right hand raised to steady the pan on her head, blocking half her sight, she couldn't have seen us, she kept walking into the road, Michael tried to veer, and we *hit* her, we struck her *down*, I heard her say "uh!" in a way I've never heard it said, never, and the jeep swerved, bounced, straightened, and kept on . . . I looked back, she was flung down on the clay pavement in the dusk, she looked lifeless. Davidia said, "Michael! Michael! She's hurt!"—"She wasn't watching!" he said angrily, going faster now. His shoulders hunched as he pushed the accelerator hard, and we were racing away from—what? A murder, perhaps. We'd never know. "Michael, Michael," Davidia said, but Michael said nothing, and she said, "Go back, go back, go back, go back," but we wouldn't go back, we couldn't—not in Africa, this hard, hard land where nobody could help that poor woman flopped probably dead in the road and where running away from this was not a mistake. The mistake was looking back at her in the first place.

No words among us now, just Davidia's sobbing, and then her silence. Michael drove a bit more soberly as we skirted the border, heading north. If we didn't find our hole soon we'd come to South Sudan. The surface got terrible. I'm not sure it was still a road. We came into a village, and the guide muttered in Michael's ear, and we went quite slowly now. Michael switched off the headlamps—he was only using the parking lights anyway—"Let's enjoy the moon!" It was just past half-full, with that lopsided swollen face, that smile at the corner of its mouth. People strolled around under its strange orange glow. Kids played tag as if it were daytime. We went slower than the pedestrians through this crowded twilight, this thickly human evening. Sudden laughter from a hut, like a soprano chorus. What have they got to laugh about? Bikes without headlights floating out of the dimness. A man leans against a shack, cupping the tiny light of a cell phone to his ear.

The guide said, "Stop." He got out, shut the door, walked around to Michael's window and spoke low.

Michael told me, "Give him fifty."

"Not till we're in Congo."

"We're here. This is Congo."

"I thought you said one hundred."

"He's quitting early. Just fifty."

I handed Michael a bill. The man folded it up small, then turned away and walked toward a hut, crying softly, "Hallooo."

"Who's coming up front—Nair?" Michael asked.

"I guess I am," I said more or less to Davidia. Her face was invisible. For the last two hours she'd said not a word. We left the village behind and lurched along a half kilometer farther and stopped.

Michael said, "The main road's over that way, but we'll never find it till we have some daylight." He fiddled with his watch. "Set your time backward one hour. We've crossed into another zone."

We sat in the car saying nothing, thinking and feeling nothing, or trying not to, while the weather changed and the stars disappeared. The moon burned right through the overcast with a curious effect, seeming to hang just a few meters above us while the clouds lay behind it, much higher in the sky. Michael switched off the engine. We heard a multitude of insects ringing all around us like finger cymbals. The ringing stopped. Raindrops exploded on the roof and streaked down the dirty windshield.

Stupid, stupid Michael said, "Congo! Here, we're not in any trouble."

[OCT 16 2AM]

How much time do I have to catch you up? They won't move us tonight, surely. The party's over and everybody's snoring, sleeping on top of their rifles. The only one awake with me is a radio somewhere—a DJ talking French full-speed and spinning American country music. And two or three mosquitoes making their rounds. Very few mosquitoes at these East African altitudes, though when Michael and Davidia and I came aground in the dark just inside the Congo border, he, Michael—to pick up the journey again—said, "Many voices on the air tonight," and rolled up the windows against the insects, because as a child he suffered malaria and a mosquito is the only thing on earth, I believe, that scares him.

The car was stifling. I slept, or only suffocated—I saw the woman in the road in more detail, the wrap that covered all but her arms and shoulders in a pattern red or purple, in the dusk it could have been either, and her basin of ants rolling on its edge away from her like a toy, and she lay there as limp as her towel—the white cloth, that is, she'd rolled into a bun to cushion her head—stretched out straight beside her.

Sometime in the night came Michael's voice: "I'm moving."

We were both awake I'm sure, Davidia and I.

"It's very subtle. But there is definitely movement."

Davidia said, "Michael, quiet."

"I'm sliding down. I'm sliding off."

"Sshh."

"I don't know what I'm going to turn into once I'm on the floor."

She: "To hell with this. To hell with you."

"I itch all over."

"Don't start your scratching. Don't scratch."

He squirmed and clawed at his ribs, elbows knocking the steering wheel. "I'm in a cocoon. What will I be when I come out?"

Davidia said, "He's going mad. We'll be holding him down while he screams bloody murder before it's over."

"I'm coming out of my skin!" he screamed. Writhing. He bumped the horn and it honked and we all jumped, and then he got hold of himself and we got quiet again.

When daylight came we found ourselves parked behind a church in the middle of a field, a big crumbling adobe building, salmon-pink, its tin roof corroded red. Beyond it lay a proper dirt road and a collection of low buildings, dark inside, the wind blowing through. But pots steamed and fry pans sizzled on cookfires all around. Without talking about it the three of us got out of the car and made our way toward the possibility of breakfast. I watched Davidia walk. Her long African skirt swayed and the hem danced around her feet as she floated ahead of me. People wandered around, others were just waking up, crawling from under a couple of lorries, dragging their straw mats behind them. Nobody remarked on us. Michael found us some corn cakes and hot tea served in plastic water bottles. He said, "Last night I became a lizard. Now I know what we have to do."

He went exploring, running his electric clippers over his scalp and his cheeks and his jaw as he walked around talking to folks.

Davidia and I sat on a bench outside a shack called The Best Lucky Saloon and she said, "Boomelay boomelay bommelay boom and all that."—"What?"—"Vachel Lindsay. Or Edna St. Vincent Millay or somebody."—"Oh."—"It's a poem about the Congo."—"Oh." We watched a woman sitting on a stool, working on the hairdo of a little girl sitting on the ground between her knees, while behind her, standing, another woman worked on *her* hair . . . The buildings and shacks were gray and brown, everything streaked with red mud. I recall three green power poles, one broken and leaning and held up apparently by the wires alone.

Michael came back with several bread rolls for each of us and said, "Some lizards can fly, so you pick up information if you become one," and went away again.

Davidia said to me, "You haven't seen this before?"

"What—seen him go through magical transformations, you mean, in the jungle night?"

"Well," she said, "when you put it that way"—she was kicking at a rock—"then it sounds as troubling as it really is."

"Maybe it's a chemical problem. Are you taking something for malaria?"

"Once a day. It's called Lariam."

"Lariam causes nightmares. I take doxycycline."

"You said 'transformations in the jungle night'—but where's the jungle?"

"The people cut it all down. They burned it to cook breakfast, mostly. And to make way for planting."

A hundred years ago it would have taken an hour to hack through ten meters of undergrowth. Now huts and footpaths and small gardens cover the hills. By 9:00 a.m. we were passing among them, back on the road, driving on the right side now instead of the left. Within 20 minutes we had a flat tire.

Very briskly Michael raised the car on a jack and attacked the nuts with a tool and got on the spare—a different-colored wheel and a wrong-sized tire lacking any tread at all.

We saw very few motorized vehicles. An occasional motorcycle, an occasional SUV, always, it seemed, stenciled with a corporate or NGO acronym. Passenger busses coming like racecars, nearly capsizing as they careened around the curves toward us, slinging dust bombs from under the wheels. A few lorries bearing cargo, laboring slowly; other lorries with smashed faces dragged among the trees and abandoned. Many, many pedestrians strolling on the margin or crossing side to side, looking up from their daydreams only at the sound of a horn. It was the holiday of sacrifice, Eid al-Adha, and Muslims walked on both sides of the road, some of the women lugging prayer mats as big as house rugs.

The point is, our Land Cruiser stood out, and we couldn't

possibly face any officials. Before we reached any sizeable town, Michael drove off the road to detour, along little more than footpaths, down into gulleys, through patches of agriculture, knocking over stalks of corn and bushes of marijuana to get around the checkpoints and then back onto the real road, along which he sped as if he hadn't only yesterday slammed this jeep into tragedy, again proceeding African style, all honking, no braking. A little boy ran right in front of the car, running at top speed as if hurrying to get killed. Michael swerved in time, mashing the horn and crying out the window in English to the boy's family, "Beat that child, beat that child!" I watched to the side, keeping my eyes off the future. The fields were a light green, the color of springtime in the temperate zones, soft and even-looking, with here and there the slow white smoke of trash fires strung over them like mist. Late that day Michael pointed at the hazy distance and claimed he saw the hills of his childhood, the Happy Mountains, called by the missionary James Hannington, in frustration and disgust, the Laughing Monsters, and Michael told us of a forest in those mountains "where you'll find pine trees about a dozen meters in their height, Nair. Bunches of ten evergreens, fifteen, twenty or more together. What do you call a bunch of trees—a copse? Copses of pines about a dozen meters in height, Nair. And these aren't common evergreens, but their needles are actually made of precious gold. And you can gather all the needles you want, but if you get pricked by one, and it draws blood—you will lose your soul. A devil comes instantly at the smell of your blood, and snatches your soul right—out—of your heart. Remember," he said, "when I told you never to have anything to do with the voodoo? Now you're going to find out why."

"Michael," I said, "was it your people who martyred Hannington?" and he only said, "Hannington was stabbed in the side with a spear like Jesus Christ."

The wedding would be blended into the Burning of the Blood, a weeklong ceremony, he said, "when we put away the bad blood of the war, and drink the new blood of peace. I tell you it is an orgy! Many babies are made. A boy conceived in that week will be a man of peace among his people. But only within wedlock. No bastard can be a man of peace."

At one point, as the dusk fell on us, he said, "Any moment now we'll reach Newada Mountain. Tear out my eyes, and I could find it by my heart."

We turned onto a road that got muddier and muddier each kilometer until we were just mushing along through patches of gumbo separated by horrifyingly slick hard flats, but at least it wasn't raining. "Fifteen kilometers more to Newada Mountain," Michael announced, and after a couple dozen kilometers, three dozen, many more than fifteen, certainly, we took a shortcut, a footpath that delivered us into a wasteland, a stinking bog of red gumbo, the sort of mud you can't stop in, even with four-wheel drive, or you'll sink and never get going again. By full nightfall we'd determined that the stink came not from the bog, but from our vehicle. "I smell petrol," Michael said, and the engine began to miss. "I'm not sure about the fuel pump," Michael said, and the engine died. He cut the headlamps, and in the blackness quite vividly I perceived how an English missionary like

James Hannington might have stood up to his buttocks in this sludge and wept, and heard the mountains laughing.

The dead engine gave out small noises as it cooled. With the headlamps switched off we could measure the darkness, which was deep and thick, without moon or stars. Every now and then the frogs started up all around, and then stopped. From far off came a wild, syncopating percussion.

Davidia said, "Are those jungle drums?"

"Probably someone's idea of a disco," Michael said.

"Well—let's go," she said, but we all three felt the impossibility of moving off on foot into the dark and the muck. Michael closed the windows and we slept the same suffocated sleep as the night before.

And woke at dawn in the foundered jeep, with no better plan than to get out of it and pee.

Michael and I stood on the driver's side, Davidia squatted on the other. We'd arrived, we now realized, nearly at the limit of the red muddy lowland, at the feet of the mountains we'd seen by day, within sight of a place of twisted trees and lopsided shacks.

"Take your packs," Michael said. "Walk soft."

He meant us to understand that by a light tread on the superficial hard spots we might not break through into the gunk, although in many spots we broke through anyway. By tacking in search of better footing we spent half an hour making a few hundred meters.

The village lay between a field of corn and a banana grove. Michael had called it exactly right—the main shack, among squat huts and other shanties, was the Biggest Club Disco, with a generator on the ground outside, not running.

Michael took a tour while Davidia and I sat on a bench and watched the village wake up, men and women fussing over cookfires beside the huts, children, chickens, goats, all going softly and talking low in the chilly dawn. Michael turned up with three Cokes and quite a few biscuits wrapped in a page of the *Monitor*, a Ugandan newspaper, and said, "Watch these people. We don't know their hearts."

"Why don't you just say they're not your tribe?"

"It's more complicated than that."

"No it isn't," I said. "Is this your clan, or not?"

"All right, the simple answer is yes—they're speaking my dialect, but it's not my close family. It's not the right time to reveal myself."

"Who do you think you are? Long-lost Ulysses?" Then I felt embarrassed for him. I could see by his look that he thought exactly that. "Michael, is this Newada Mountain?"

"By my reckoning, it's very near."

Davidia wasn't suffering any of this. "Get us some real food," she told him.

"Sit there," he said, as if we weren't already slumped side by side on the bench.

When he'd gone I moved close to her, hip touching hip. I said, "He's using you for something. Something mystical, superstitious."

"Like?"

"I don't know. Kidnapping one of the gods and coercing the others to . . . rearrange the fate of us all."

She made a sort of barking noise, with tears in her eyes. "You're crazy."

"As crazy as he is?"

"No. Once in a while."

"It's time I got you out of here."

"You don't have to say it twice."

"Then let's go."

"Go how?"

"We'll walk."

"Where?"

"Uganda's that way—east."

"How far?"

"I don't know. But it isn't getting any closer while we sit here."

"What will he do?"

"Nothing. He can't hold us at gunpoint."

"Why not?"

"Because he hasn't got a gun."

Something was happening, suddenly, to every person in the village—as if they choked on poisonous fumes—and their voices got loud, and we heard a vehicle in the distance. Davidia asked me what was wrong, who was coming, what kind of car. "I don't know," I said, "but I don't give a shit—we'll hitch a ride out of here or kill them and take the fucking thing." Then we heard other engines, several vehicles, none of them visible yet. Somebody had a gun: one shot, two, three . . . then the rest of a clip. At that point our own jeep, three hundred meters away and to the right of us, burst into silent brightness—the boom of the explosion came a second later.

Davidia and I stood up simultaneously from the bench. We watched a white pickup truck scurrying across the landscape at a tangent to us, driving hysterical villagers before it, sparks of rifle fire bursting from the passenger window and soldiers standing up in the back and firing too, when they could manage it, as they bounced and swayed and hung on.

I turned toward the nearest copse of larger trees, and discovered that it was besieged by other vehicles. I felt relief when Michael came toward us in a hurry calling, "Let's go, let's go, let's go."

The banana grove seemed a possibility. Anywhere, really. We proceeded in a sort of innocent, unprovoked manner, nothing wrong here, just walking.

We entered the grove. Behind us came a hush, then a man's rapid voice, many gunshots, and the uninterrupted keening of a woman somewhere, and soon the whole village, it seemed, was crying out, some of them screeching like birds, some bawling, some moaning low. Every child sounded like every other child.

As soon as we'd put a little distance between us and the din of souls in the clearing, I sat on the edge of a pile of adobe bricks and wrapped my arms around my middle. "My stomach's a sack of vomit."

"I'll give you ten seconds. Then double-time."

"Where's Davidia?"

"I'm right here." She was behind me.

A woman burst onto the path ahead of us with eyes like headlights, running with her hands high in the air. Bullets tugged at the banana leaves around her.

I lost my head. I see that now. We'd moved a hundred meters along this path, breathing hard, our steps pounding, before I formed any clear intention of getting up and running. Of my panicked state I remember only others panicking, the faces of tiny children swollen into cartoon caricature, the long wet lashes and pouting lips and baby cheeks and the teardrops exploding like molten gobs in the air around their heads. I remember shoes left behind on the ground—flip-flops, slippers, whatever's hard to run in.

Michael collided with my back, gripped each of my elbows from behind, and propelled me along. Davidia kept pace, clawed at our clothing, at the banana fronds too, and got in front of us, then away from us, and Michael steered me off the path and hugged me, stopped me.

"You can't outrun bullets."

"Yes I can!" I meant it.

He pointed amid the grove and said, "Go ten meters and get down." He watched while I obeyed, then was gone.

Multiple guns now, and many fewer voices.

I lay on my belly. A few steps from my face the grove ceased, and to the right the gumbo bog took over, and for an unquantifiable period I watched a heap of something burning out there before I understood it was our vehicle. Part of the driveshaft remained, a wheel with its tire, and around these two things only the shell, still giving out small flames, and surrounding that, the red earth steaming and smoking.

Michael came along leading Davidia by the hand.

I stood and followed them along the edge of the grove and toward a cornfield. We stopped to watch the white pickup truck charging at us, plowing down the stalks until it slid to a stop almost in our faces, a spiffy little truck with fresh gold lettering across its front windshield: ALL EYEZ ON ME. Soldiers leapt from the back of it, and the three of us walked before their guns.

We waited in front of the disco while they wrapped up

the looting. Most of the villagers had escaped—no more screams, only the soldiers' whoops, their panting and shouting, and much laughter. The young recruit responsible for us drifted some distance away, dazzled by the excitement, but rather than running, Michael and I sat Davidia on the bench and stood in front of her as camouflage because we didn't want anybody noticing us, noticing Davidia, raping Davidia—and they raped a couple of women behind the disco, a young one and her mother, who in their terror seemed almost apathetic, almost asleep, and who afterward walked away brushing the dirt from their bare arms and the fronts of their torn shifts. It took the commander a full hour to bring his troops to order. He mustered them in front of the disco, thirty or so young men in green cammy uniforms, and went from face to face lecturing bitterly, pointing often at the shreds of our Land Cruiser out in the wasteland. Apparently rape and looting were lesser crimes than blowing up a good machine.

Michael said, "Did you see the fireball? Petrol vapors. I told you the fuel pump was ruptured."

[OCT 16 6AM]

I know Michael's sleeping. He'll sleep through a barrage. I don't know where he's being kept, or Davidia. I hope they're together. I'm in the main hut with the commander, along with ten or twelve other men, the number changes, they come and go. It's a spacious hut, an open-air corral, really, with low adobe walls under a thatched roof, a cafeteria table, a tattered couch, three broken chairs.

They've got my pack, my extra clothes, passport, cash—4K in US twenties, fifties, and hundreds. They left me my Timex watch, out of contempt for the brand or perhaps for the concept of time itself. They stole my penlight too, but they've lent it back so I can write by its tiny glow.

Why take everything but the watch and the light and my ballpoint pen, and then give me this lined paper torn from a schoolroom notebook, 42 sheets of it? I've sat up all night scrawling on them because I'm too terrified to sleep. The liquor's worn off and I'm going mad. When I've filled these pages they'll be included, I suspect, with some sort of ransom demand.

The roosters are calling. Nobody's stirring yet but one person out by the latrines—a young woman in a dirty linen shift, barefoot, hardly more than a girl, hacking a trough in the earth with a vicious-looking short-handled hoe, a trough in the earth shaped, I'm afraid, quite like a grave.

[OCT 16 8AM]

The commander claims to be regular Army but could easily be lying, or just confused. His cammy uniform bears no insignia. Beneath his open tunic he wears a T-shirt with the faded emblem of a bottle on it, soda or beer. He calls himself a general, won't say his name. Drives his own little cream-colored Nissan truck, the one that says EYEZ ON ME.

He takes me for the leader, because I'm the white one.

Last night, after discovering that my bad French and his own bad English render idle conversation impossible, he nodded toward the small cassette player on his table and punched a button, and it played a song called, I believe, "Coat of Many Colors," by Dolly Parton, over and over. Just that one song, repeating. This wasn't psychological warfare, but a sincere attempt at hospitality.

This morning he shared with me his general's breakfast: strips of tripe in a broth smelling pretty much like kerosene. It took me a while to get it all down and set the bowl aside. The meal came with dessert, a sugary pudding sprinkled with the legs, if not more, of some sort of insect.

[OCT 16 12 NOON]

After breakfast, when I thought everybody was still sleeping off last night's liquor, they all jumped up on the general's shouted orders and mustered in the clearing among the huts for the very quick court martial of the recruit who blew up our Land Cruiser.

When they'd made a circle and wrestled themselves to attention, all thirty or more of them, the general's aide-de-camp, his main henchman, dragged the youngster out of a hut barefoot and stripped down to ragged gray shorts and stood him up before the fresh-dug grave. His hands were tied behind him with a winding of black rubber. Perhaps from a tire's inner tube.

I made up part of this audience of dazed, half-dressed soldiers. Davidia and Michael stood across from me. They were many feet apart. Davidia looked unhurt, unmolested. The magic of her US passport must be working.

Michael, with his Ghanaian document, enjoys no immunity. He caught my eye and turned sideways—his arms were bound behind him, but I couldn't see his hands for the press of the crowd. He smiled and shrugged.

Our general faced us taking a similar posture, hands behind his back and feet apart, and addressed the whole group briefly—in a localized French, I think—before tearing off his sunglasses and turning on the malefactor and lecturing him in the face for five or more minutes, screaming into the kid's open mouth, right down his throat. During this harangue the general's henchman strutted back and forth in his mirrored sunglasses and helmet, slapping his pistol against his palm, until it was time to push the kid to his knees and put the gun to his head. The youth wept and bawled while the general shouted him down to silence. When all was quiet, he counted down from trois!—deux!—un! and the henchman's hammer snapped on a empty chamber.

The general laughed. Then the troops all laughed too.

The general pushed his henchman aside and drew his own pistol and raised it high and pulled the slide back as if demonstrating how to cock this particular weapon and pushed the barrel hard against the kid's neck and forced him down onto his face, and bent over him like that while he sobbed into the dirt. Some of the troops exclaimed—the general would get it done! . . . He stared hard one by one at each face, saying nothing, until he'd forced them all into a state of pensive sobriety. He worked his shoulders. Shifted his stance. Planted his feet. Still playing, I felt sure of it. But the pistol was cocked, and one small mistake makes a murder, and in Africa, so the old hands assure me, the first one pops some kind of cork, and they don't quit after that.

Ten seconds passed. Once more the boy spoke out—a pitiable, wrenching sound, his face like a newborn's—trying to direct his words backward to the man about to dispatch him.

The general fired one loud shot into the sky. Again the exclamations—fooled us two times! He turned his back on the youngster and leveled the weapon at the crowd, aiming in particular at Michael Adriko's face.

Michael bared his teeth and wagged his head and played the clown. Nobody laughed. On either of his shoulders lay a black hand, but his guards seemed not to know who the general referred to when he cried in English: "That one!"

Or maybe they didn't know the words. He said that one, that one, that one until the two men unslung their rifles and prodded Michael forward to the edge of the ditch. The general held out his hand and wiggled his fingers for one of the weapons, an AK, the kind with a folding stock and a pistol grip, and he swung it around and jabbed the barrel at Michael's chest.

Michael stepped backward into the ditch and stood with the young recruit in a ball at his feet while the general put the barrel's mouth against one of Michael's eyeballs, and then the other, and then the first again. Michael dodged his head and clamped his mouth around the barrel and sucked and French-kissed it with his tongue, the whole time looking up into the general's face as if wooing a woman. Oh, Michael. If one voice laughs . . . Perhaps the general would laugh. But the general had been carried beyond his instincts and had to wait for Michael to decide what happened next. Michael drew his head back and averted his gaze, and the general seized on that as a sign of surrender and returned the rifle to its owner and stooped, hooked a hand into Michael's armpit, and helped him out of the ditch. He spoke softly to Michael, and Michael answered softly. I don't know what they said.

Another minute, and the party was over, everyone dismissed, they were taking Michael back toward the smaller huts. Apparently they kept him separate from Davidia.

As he passed, he said to me, to Davidia, to the sky's blank face—"We'll be fine. I'm talking to these people. A few of them are Kakwa, like me."

Somehow he'd not only cheated fate, but also coaxed it to lend him a cigarette, which one of his guards was lighting for him as they dragged him back to his prison. Puffing, squinting, he hopped along as if often in the habit of smoking with his hands tied behind his back.

I got close to Davidia. Before they separated us again, I said to her, "Are you all right?"

She said, "Yes. Yes. Are you?"

[OCT 16 1:30PM]

I'm back in the general's quarters. "Coat of Many Colors"—"Coat of Many Colors"—"Coat of Many Colors"—

My pen's got a fresh cartridge, but the ball keeps skipping. This encourages more deliberate penmanship.

Tina,—

Tina. I doubt you'll see me again in the flesh. I may as

well embrace candor. With every stroke of this pen I've wanted to say it: I've lost my heart to this woman. I'm in love with Davidia St. Claire. The sight of her blinds me. This morning, the nearness of her outshone everything going on among these violent men.

Right now I feel two ways. I'm grateful Davidia's all right. I'm sorry that Michael isn't dead.

FOUR

Online again—bathed and shaved and revived after eleven hours' sleep, plus three cups of coffee brewed American style—I wrote to Tina:

> You'll be hearing from the boys in Sec 4, and I suspect you've been briefed to some extent already by your own bunch.
>
> I regret your involvement, nothing else. But your involvement—deeply.
>
> I don't mean to be curt, just brief. I don't know how long I have the machine.
>
> They'll intercept this communication, I suppose,

and blackline half of it—but friends, please, let me tell her this much unredacted:

Listen, Tina, when the boys from Sec 4 come around, remember you work for the US, not NATO, not really. I'd urge you not to speak to them. In fact there's no reason why you shouldn't just go back right now to DC. Or even home to Michigan.

Thanks, chums. Thanks for letting me transmit that bit of advice.

I just want to be careful not to overstep with my hosts. Who are they? Well fuck, as we Yanks like to say, if I know. Friends of Intelligence. Meaning allies of stupidity.

That was snotty. They've been cordial. I should delete it.

—But I saw them coming for me and pressed SEND.

•

On the afternoon of the second day, my backpack, my own toiletries, and freshly laundered underwear—also my own—appeared on my bed. But not my watch.

And not my clothes. We still paraded around in red pajamas of cotton-polyester, the same material as the white sheets on our beds—not cots, but barracks beds. And we still possessed the olive socks, shorts, and undershirts they'd issued us. We'd been allowed to keep the shoes we'd arrived in.

"We" being myself and one tentmate, a Frenchman, Patrick Roux, not Patrice, a tiny man with a sparrow's face and giant horn-rim spectacles, and a five-day beard and bitten fingernails and a personal odor like that of linseed oil . . . or was my sensitive nose merely sniffing out a fake, a plant, a snitch?

The Congolese Army couldn't reach us here. I could sleep knowing I wouldn't be prodded awake with a gun barrel and then shot; though I rather expected to be greeted one morning with some delicious coffee and informed of my arrest on a charge of espionage.

•

After supper on the second night, I wrote to Tina online:

> I won't outrage you with pleas for forgiveness. I hope you hate me, actually, as much as I hate myself. And no explanation—nothing you'd understand—only this: the other day Michael asked me if I really want to go back to that boring existence. I said No.
>
> They've reviewed and returned some dozens of pages I filled by hand. None of it, apparently, impinges on their plans for world domination. If I somehow crawl free of this mess, I'll transcribe and transmit those pages to you, and I may even take time one day to set down an account of things, everything, beginning—17 days ago? Really, only 17 days?
>
> They've made a few things clear. I'll get one hour's online access per day, sending to NIIA recipient(s) only (including you), and I'd better be careful not to compromise in any serious way what they're up to down here—or else what? They'll take away my red pajamas?
>
> Right now I can tell you I'm still in Africa. Behind loop-de-loops of razor concertina wire, shiny

and new. Behind barricades four sandbags thick and nearly four meters high.

I suppose they'll redact this too, but for what it's worth: I'm here thanks, I'm sure, to Davidia St. Claire, thanks to her relation with the US Tenth Special Forces Group, in whose hands I now find myself. I believe yesterday I caught a glimpse of their fearless leader, Col. George Thiebes himself, out there on the grounds. Commander of the whole 10th. I'm pretty sure I was meant to.

This isn't a prison. My tentmate and I are the only ones in red pajamas. The setup for the fifty or so African detainees (they wear white) seems make-shift and temporary—they're rounded up and soon released.

Our pajamas say "Nair" and "Roux"—handwritten with textile markers—but none of the personnel wear name tags on their utilities or have names stenciled on their T-shirts.

Even during meals, Roux removes his glasses frequently and spends a lot of time breathing on the lenses and polishing them with his shirttail. He speaks to me only in French but rolls his *r*'s like a Spaniard. I gather he returned from business in Marseilles to find that his wife, a Congolese, had gone missing, and while running around looking for her he did something, he can't guess what, to bring himself in conflict with the American dream.

Nobody stops me from having a walk around, but whenever I do, one or more large enlisted men go walking around the same places.

Davidia must still be here. I have no reason to believe they've taken her elsewhere.

Michael Adriko is elsewhere. He never got here. He's gone. He got away.

•

After two days' grilling, I got a break.

Off-line, I finished transcribing the handwritten letter to Tina. The notebook pages ended with this quick entry:

> *I've slept two hours with my face on the table and just woke up to find everything changed. The general returned my pack and clothes and even several hundred of my 4K dollars—all the twenties.*
>
> *Michael's sitting in the back of the general's pickup—hands unbound. I saw Davidia getting in the front. The day has turned. Whether it turns upside down I*
>
> *Much activity—time to go—*
>
> . . . All right, Tina, there you have it. My rise from terrified prisoner to confused detainee.
>
> Michael or Davidia must have told the Congolese Army about her connection with the 10th Special Forces. And only about Davidia's connection, surely, because when Michael disappeared, nobody cared.
>
> Last time I saw Michael I was getting in the truck, up front, with the Congolese so-called general and Davidia. Michael leaned over the rail, nearly into my window, and handed me a pellet of chewing gum. "Here. Keep yourself busy."

When we made our rendezvous that night, it was like a magic trick. During a rain, the men in the back of the general's pickup had covered themselves with a dark plastic tarp. They whipped the tarp off. Michael had vanished.

Our escort were three US infantry Nissan pickups, just like our general's, only olive rather than white.

As Davidia and I boarded, one of the youngsters who'd guarded us said to me, "Newada Mountain."

"Yes?"

"I am from there. I am Kakwa."

"Yes?"

"Your friend is there."

"Michael? My African friend?"

"Yes. He left to Newada Mountain."

"Oh!" I said—getting it for the first time—"New Water Mountain."

As for lately, Tina: no activity to report. I've spent the day in idleness, in limbo, in hope. I've made a proposal, and wheels may be turning. We just might forge an arrangement. In any case, they haven't said no, and they've given me a day off. I can use one—my head still spins, and I slept very little last night, and before that I had no appetite for dinner, as my lunch was interrupted when this American, wow, a genuine asshole—attached to NIIA I suppose, but he withheld identification—dropped out of the sky.

I was sitting at a table with Patrick Roux, my tentmate and alleged fellow detainee, when we heard what must have been this new man's chopper landing but thought nothing of it, choppers come and go. Ten minutes later he entered and bumped across the cafeteria like a blimpy cartoon animal, I mean in a state of personal awkwardness, as if balancing a stack of plates, but he carried only his hands before him, at chest level. A blue checked shirt, khaki pants, brown loafers. "Come and talk to me."—And I said, "No." He had a fringe of brown hair with a big bald spot. He had fat cheeks and soulful, angry eyes. Reasonably young, mid-thirties.

He stood by my place leaning on the table and looking down at me until a sergeant and a private came and lifted me by either arm from behind. As they quick-marched me out, he went over to the serving line, apparently for some lunch.

Online, just before I pressed SEND, I added:

The soldiers took me to a tent, and the sergeant left, and the private stood at ease by the tent fly, and I sat on one half of the furniture, that is, on one of two folding chairs.

The sergeant returned with a chair of his own, unfolded it, and sat down and stared at me. Together we waited thirty minutes for my first interrogator.

I said nothing, and the sergeant said nothing.

He was present every minute of every session, and he always said nothing, and he never stopped staring.

•

My answers had to come fast. He who hesitates is lying.

"We've been getting a lot of NTRs from you."

"We?"

"Your reports have been forwarded to us. They were all NTRs."

"If there's nothing to report, that's what I report. Would you rather I make things up?"

"Why would you transmit two identical NTRs with a thirty-second interval between them?"

My stomach sank down to my groin. It irritated me that I couldn't control my breath.

"On October second you sent two NTRs in a row from the Freetown facility, thirty seconds apart. Why is that?"

"It was my initial utilization of the equipment. I chose to double up."

"But on October eleventh you sent an NTR from the Arua station. Weren't you utilizing that equipment for the first time?"

"It didn't seem necessary to be redundant. I had confidence in the equipment because the setup there seemed more robust—was obviously more robust."

"Why don't you go Danish if you're working Danish?"

"Pardon?"

"If you're working as a Dane, why don't you travel as a Dane?"

"I thought I was working for NATO."

"You're an army captain."

"Yes."

"In whose army?"

"Denmark."

"Flashing a US passport."

"A Danish passport is something of a risk, because I hardly speak Danish at all. It makes me look bogus."

"Two NTRs thirty seconds apart—isn't that a pretty crude and obvious signal?"

He was right. I kept quiet.

"Who intercepted that crude and obvious signal? Who was it actually meant for?"

"This is boring. Can't we just talk?"

"I see you're in red."

"You're noticing only now?"

"White is for the grown-ups. Red is for the noncompliant. Gitmo protocol."

"Guantánamo Bay?"

"Yes."

"All those nifty short forms—I hate them."

"Give us a location on Michael Adriko."

Here I counted to five before admitting, "I've lost him."

"General location. Uganda? Congo?"

"Congo."

"East? West?"

"East."

"Close to here?"

"I could only guess."

"Then do so."

"I believe he has reason to be in the area."

"You had him, you lost him, he's reachable. We should know that. Isn't that something to report?"

"From what facility? We've been in the bush."

"I'd call it something to report."

I raised a middle finger. "Report this."

"Believe me, I will."

"Good."

"Now we're getting somewhere," he said. "Do you smoke?"

"No."

"Smoke pot? Opium?"

"Never."

"Which one?"

"Cut it out."

"What about alcohol?"

"Yes."

"Correct. You were reported drunk in the restaurant of the Papa Leone there in Freetown on . . ." He consulted his notepad.

Fucking Horst. Old Bruno. "The evening of the sixth," I said.

"So you agree."

"I agree on the date. Not on my condition. I didn't take a Breathalyzer."

"What about when you sent the meltdown message, rockets up your ass and 'go fuck yourselves' and all that, were you drunk?"

"I'm sober now. Go fuck yourself."

He said, "Captain Nair, in March of 2033 they'll give me a gold watch, and I can retire. Till then I've got nothing to do but this."

"I'm through answering questions."

"As you wish. But you and I will stay right here."

"When can I see an attorney?"

"As your legal status evolves, you'll be afforded that opportunity."

"And my legal status is—what?"

"Evolving. In accordance with the progress of this interview."

"Well, the progress has stopped. When can I leave?"

"Right now you're being detained without recourse to counsel under US antiterrorism laws."

"Which law in particular?"

"You can expect to be informed of that as your status evolves."

"Okay. Suppose this interview sails smoothly along. What can you offer me?"

"A good listener."

"Then I'll be the one to make the offer," I said. "I'm going to tell you everything, and then I expect you to bring in somebody higher up. Somebody who can deal."

"I'm not considering any offers."

"Then I assume you're not authorized."

"I don't recommend you make assumptions."

"But surely you can send me up the chain."

"Also an assumption."

"Fine. Offer withdrawn. Let the silence begin."

Our bodyguard, the sergeant, was one to emulate. On taking his seat he'd rested his hands on his knees, and he hadn't disturbed them since.

Within half a minute I had to wipe sweat from my upper lip. Why had I begun this contest? And did it matter what I told them? They're only digging for lies, and when they turn up the truth they brush it aside and go on digging, stupid as dogs.

The interrogator had the sense not to let it go on. He

looked at his wristwatch, which might have been platinum. "Here's an idea, Captain Nair. Why don't you repeat your offer, and why don't I accept it?"

•

Our tent had a good rubber roof without leaks. A strip of mosquito gauze running under the eaves let in the searing light all night, the disorienting yellow-ochre sunshine without shadows. Except for the microwave and satellite towers the base resembled an expanse of sacred aboriginal rubble, sandbag bunkers, Quonset huts emerging from mounds of earth bulldozed against them, and in the midst of it all two monumental generators that never stopped. No fuel or water reservoirs in evidence—they must have been buried. An acre of trucks and fighting vehicles, a hangar like a small mountain, a helicopter bull's-eye. Mornings and evenings a live bugler, not a recording, blew reveille and taps.

Our sandbag perimeter could have accommodated three more tents, but ours stood alone. My tentmate liked to sit on the wall and stare across the way at the chain-link enclosure full of Africans, nearly fifty of them, Lord's Resistance, I should think, or collaborators, women on the north side, men on the south. No children. The men spent their time right against the divider, fingers curled on the wire, laughing and talking, while the women formed a single clump on the other side, never looking at the men. Once in a while a downpour drove them all under blue plastic canopies strung up in the corners. Quarrels erupted often among the women. I never heard any voice that sounded like Davidia's.

Patrick thought he might spot his wife among them, so he said. Still paying out this line. I didn't buy it.

We took our meals with everyone else. Officers and enlisted men ate together in a large Quonset along with civilian guests and Special Ops helicopter crews and detainees from NATO countries, of which Patrick and I were the only ones, the only people modeling red pajamas.

The Special Activities Division sees some sort of advantage, I think, in starting the questions when your fork is halfway to your mouth. Just grab you up, goodbye hamburger sandwich, and it's off to the interrogator.

This one was new. And that was good.

•

We met in a Quonset hut, in an office with a desk, two aluminum dining chairs, and some empty cardboard boxes and a cardboard barrel of MREs I could have stood in up to my neck. "Meal Rammed in an Envelope," he said. "Care to suck one down?" I declined. He served me black coffee. I could have chosen tea and milk.

I said, "Where's Sergeant Stone today?"

"Sergeant Stone?"

"I don't know if his name was Stone, but he certainly seemed to be made of it."

"No sergeants here."

"He never introduced himself. Neither did the civilian."

"Under current regulations, that's not a requirement."

"But under the circumstances, it might be courteous."

"Sure. Agreed."

"So—who are you?"

"Let's skip over the courtesies for now. Can I suggest we do that, without irritating the shit out of you?"

I was too irritated to answer.

He used a lot of motions getting a bag of tea into a cup. He seemed older than the first one, but in a way he looked younger, looked barbered and tailored, in dark trousers, a nice white shirt—I wouldn't know silk, but it might have been—and cuff links. He looked the way I try to look.

He sat down facing me with our knees nearly touching. We observed each other's manner of drinking from a cup.

"Captain Nair, I'd like your opinion."

"I'm full of opinions."

"Good. Well. In the fullness of your opinion—does all this you've been telling us the last couple of days sound like a desperate, unbelievable lie?"

I counted to three. "Yes." Counted again. "Now can I ask you a question?" Silence. "Where are you going?"

"I'm not going anywhere."

"Why not?"

He sipped his tea.

"In case I'm telling the truth."

He drained his cup. "Or in case you stop lying. More coffee?"

"No, thanks."

He stood and set our cups aside and pulled his chair behind his desk and sat down. "I've reviewed all your written material," he said, opening a drawer and taking out a manila file folder.

"Yes."

He laid it apart before him. Printed e-mails, and my long note to Tina. "The Congolese Army threw you quite a party."

"Yes."

"Stressful."

"Yes."

He spent a few minutes perusing the pages of the letter, pages crusty from sweat and tears. "Sometimes I wish I had the balls to say this stuff. I don't even have the balls to think it."

I didn't reply.

"Another way of putting it is that we're seeing a lot of anger, and that's not characteristic of our expectations. No matter what the level of stress."

"I don't deny it—lately I've been out of sorts."

"Sure, that's another way to put it. If you think all this is funny."

"Well, I was dispatched to this region on an assignment, and now two weeks later I'm being dealt with as some kind of terrorist."

"I think you're regarded as absent from your assignment."

"But I'm not absent, I'm present. Here I am, waiting to get back to work."

"A Special Forces attaché goes AWOL, starts making alarming noises about enriched uranium. You're sent to make contact, deliver one report that you've done so, and you immediately go silent." He raised a printed e-mail by two corners and faced it toward me. "Until this maniac salvo."

"I've been pursuing my assignment according to my best judgment."

"And this meltdown message? 'Cunts' and such?"

"Everybody likes to quote that one."

"I know. It's very compelling. But why did you send it?"

"Theater," I said.

"Really."

"I'm dealing with some rogue Mossad agents. I had to make it look good."

"A rogue Mossad agent, you're saying, was sitting beside you while you transmitted insults to your NATO colleagues."

"Didn't the last guy tape our interviews? Yes? Have you heard them?"

"I've read highlights of the transcript."

"Then if you want the details, you can read the whole thing. Don't ask me to rehash."

"And all of this, the crazy transmission, tossing your commo equipment, getting rounded up by the Congolese Army, all of this was in fulfillment of your superiors' request that you keep a close eye on this fellow. And you say your mission's momentum has declined sharply. And you propose a strategy to reboot."

"Yes."

He sat back with an empty-handed shrug. Shaking his head. Smiling. "Hard to know what to make of all this."

"I want to ask about Davidia St. Claire."

"On that subject I've got nothing to share with you. I mean really—I just don't know. But she's not in any trouble. I'd be more concerned about the one you sent the notes to. Tina? Is that her name?"

"You can read the name right there. I can read it, upside down."

"This would be Tina Huntington. Works for us in Amsterdam."

"Who's you?"

"Who—me?"

"You say us. Who's us?"

We both laughed.

"We the Americans, from the USA," he said.

"Right. She works for you. You're NATO?"

"Nope. I'm a US naval attaché."

"Rank?"

"I'm attached. Not in. Just attached."

"So you don't need an ocean."

"I have an ocean. I'm actually assigned to a ship."

"In the Indian Ocean? African Atlantic?"

"Well, it moves around. It has propellers."

"A carrier?"

"Naw. A command ship. Floating office complex. Just about a luxury liner. USSOCOM."

"I don't know what that is."

"USSOCOM? US Special Operations Command. The ship is the regional command center."

"For this region."

"Yes."

"Meaning—DR Congo? East Africa?"

"For AFRICOM. Africa. The whole continent."

I felt, suddenly, in love. I leaned closer to study his face. "Who are you?"

"I'm the person who can deal."

"You still don't have a name?"

"The name I have is Susan Rice."

"You're not black enough to be Susan Rice."

"Plus, she's a woman."

"I was getting round to that."

"I'm the closest thing to Susan Rice."

She was the current national security advisor in the White House. The queen, in other words, of the secrets and the dark.

He placed his hands on the desk before him. He liked this part. "Well, Captain Nair, you've rubbed the right lantern."

•

Patrick Roux and I sat on our sandbag wall observing a gang of men creating more sandbags—not all men, actually. We often saw women wearing US uniforms. And of course we saw women among the white-garbed African prisoners. Never any kind of female civilian. Never Davidia.

In the motor lot I counted twenty-two Nissan pickups with canopy shells. One dozen Humvees. Four Stryker fighting vehicles, each worth millions. The helicopter hangar probably housed a chopper big enough to devour them all.

I said to Patrick, "This was more amusing when it was science fiction."

He appeared not to comprehend.

The sandbag detail worked in three-person teams—the digger, the sacker, the stacker—filling bags from a heap of dirt and loading them onto a flatbed truck. I remembered reading, as a child, during the first Gulf War, that in order to supply such sacks for their emplacements the Yanks were shipping thousands of tons of American sand across the seas to the Arabian Desert.

Within our perimeter we had a chemical port-a-potty and a vestibule containing a proper shower that ran hot water up from under the ground. Always hot. You couldn't run it out.

The mess served excellent fare. Real eggs, real potatoes, American meat. In the mornings we smelled the pastries baking.

We had two sets each of the red pajamas, underwear, bedsheets, and towels, and our laundry was collected by enlisted personnel and returned clean eight hours later. That we made our own beds began to seem unreasonable.

•

For nearly an hour I sat alone. When my host arrived he didn't sit down, hardly entered his own office. "I've gone over the transcripts in detail."

"Very good," I said, but he'd already left the room again.

In five minutes he returned, shut the door, and occupied his desk. I waited for an offer of coffee. He plunged into a period of meditation in the manner of Sherlock Holmes, elbows on the table, fingertips on his temples.

"What makes you think we'd pay you off and let you stroll out of here?"

"You'll have to help me figure that out."

Silence.

"I'll need a convincing story."

Silence.

"But if I turn up with a good enough story, and if I've got a bag of money to vouch for it, then the thing is in motion again, and the direction of that motion is toward something that has to be taken extremely seriously. Don't you think?"

"We're taking it seriously. No matter how unlikely. This shit story from Michael Adriko—Adriko? Or Adriko."

"Accent on the second syllable. Adriko."

"A ton or more of HEU. You're really alleging that?"

"I can only personally vouch for the existence of two kilos, approximately—judging by its weight in my hand."

"You held it in your hand."

"I did so. Yes." He was silent. "I don't know anything about nuclear devices or their manufacture." Silent. "I'm wondering, though, if a couple of kilos wouldn't go a long way." I wished I'd stop talking, but his silence was working on me. "I mean in terms of explosive capability. I have no explosives training. But possible damage. Destructive potential." Still silent. "So even if two kilos is all he's got—"

"Would you submit to a polygraph?"

"Oh. Well. Where—here? When?"

"It wouldn't be hard to arrange. Can I arrange it?"

"Of course. If it amuses you, fine, sure, but I mean—I can tell you now, you'll get an Inconclusive. I mean to say—I've been telling so many lies and listening to so many lies until I don't know what's true and what's false. And we're in Africa, you realize"—shut up shut up, I told myself, shut *up*—"and you realize it's all myths and legends here, and lies, and rumors. You realize that." I bit down on my tongue, and that worked.

He waited, but I was done.

"All right. Excuse me for just a minute. Help yourself to coffee. Ten minutes max." He left the door halfway open behind him.

The coffee urn waited within my reach. I drew myself a cup—yesterday's, room temperature. I couldn't form a useful thought. I kept tasting the coffee, expecting it to turn hot and fresh. Without a watch I could only guess, but it seemed rather closer to thirty minutes than ten.

When he came back in, he drew himself a cup too and sat behind his desk, sipped once, said, "Jesus," and then went silent.

He interrupted his thoughts only once to say, "No polygraph."

He got up and went to the door and called out, "Clyde?" and sat down behind his desk again. "Take these cups, will you?" he said to the private who arrived. "And bring us a fresh service. Not the whole bucket. Just a carafe or something, okay? Leave the door open."

The silence resumed. I had the impression nothing in the world could happen until we had coffee.

"I'm authorized to tell you Davidia St. Claire is on her way home."

"Oh . . ."

"You can assume she's been debriefed. Queried. Meticulously."

"You mean she's already left?"

"Let's concentrate on the people in this room."

"Just tell me—is she gone?"

"If she's not, she will be soon." The private took a step into the room and paused. "Thank you, Clyde. Is it Clyde?"

"Yes, sir."

"Thanks. Pull the door shut as you leave." To me he said, "I want to hear you say it." He let the carafe languish on his desk. Poured no coffee. "I want to hear exactly what you're proposing."

"Well, just what you said a few minutes ago, what you suggested."

"Which is?"

"That you pay me off and let me stroll out of here. And I get back to what I was doing, and see if the deal is still in motion, or if the deal can be started up again, and see if we can bring the parties together as arranged."

"The parties to this proposed, this alleged, this fucking unprecedented criminal conspiracy."

"Yes. Those parties."

"You, and these Israelis, and the people Sergeant Adriko represents. If such exist."

"That would be the objective."

"A sting operation."

"That sounds," I agreed, "like the applicable terminology."

"I think we've already deployed the applicable terms, fairy tale, for instance, and bullshit, what else, God," he said, "there's not a shred of doubt in my mind. You are fucking with us."

"And yet—here we are."

"I can't deny it. Since nine-eleven, chasing myths and fairy tales has turned into a serious business. An industry. A lucrative one."

"Are we talking price now?"

"What a silly, silly man."

"But if we were."

"Then I suppose this would be the moment when you say a number."

"They want two million."

"Cash? Or account?"

"Gold."

"They expect gold?"

"Would that be possible?"

"Gold. What's the price of gold these days?"

"Around forty-five a kilo, US."

"Forty-five thousand. So, forty-some kilos. Forty-four plus."

"Call it forty-five."

"Forty-five kilos of gold."

"Could you do it?"

The look in his eyes made me sorry for him. "Do you want to hear the truth?"

"Yes."

"We can do anything."

•

Early afternoon. I lay on my bed. I heard the sound of a helicopter coming down.

The walls of the tent rippled. Then they convulsed. I determined to stay inside and avoid the dust, but I was visited with an intuition. I knew. I went outside.

I stood by the sandbag hedge and watched the man I still believe to have been Colonel Thiebes, now in officer's dress, heading for the chopper as it swayed in its descent, a duffel grip in his left hand, his right hand cupping the elbow of Davidia St. Claire.

Davidia and her protector stopped and let the red cloud overwhelm them while the machine completed its landing. It was a utility helicopter, but not a Black Hawk, something smaller, I don't know what kind. Davidia leaned toward its skis as they felt for the ground. She concentrated on that vision. No backward glance. The chopper had hardly touched down before they were in motion toward it.

I ran to overtake her. I called her name. She couldn't hear me for the roar of the blades. I called again—"Davidia!" I screamed it many times over.

I gave up running and turned my back against the dust. In a few seconds the wind fell off and the noise got smaller. The craft must have been traveling low, because when I looked around again I could hear it, but I couldn't find it in the sky.

I went back into the tent and closed and zipped the flap and sat on my bed, blinking my eyes and beating the dirt from my hair hand over hand.

•

I felt a touch on my shoulder, and I woke up frightened. It was dark, quiet—very late.

Patrick Roux said, "These are your clothes."

He sat there in our only chair. I could see he held something in his lap. "It's time to get dressed."

He was speaking Danish.

"What?"

"It's time to go. Right now the way is open."

"Wait. Wait . . . *what*?"

"It's time to go. Just take some items for grooming. What you can fit in your pockets. Here's your wristwatch back."

Great joy powered me out of bed. "You fucker," I said. "I knew it."

"You prefer English?" he said in English.

"Or German," I said. "I went to Swiss schools. The truth is I hardly speak Danish at all. Is this my shirt? I went to English-speaking schools."

"We have six more minutes."

"They've shrunk my shirt."

"Let's be prompt."

•

When I'd kicked my pajamas aside and dressed and was all ready to go, we delayed, I on my bed, Patrick in the chair, with nothing to do, it seemed, but listen to the rumble of the generators and the giant buzzing of the floodlights outside. He peered at his wristwatch. My own watch, the cheap dependable Timex, read 1:15 a.m.

After two minutes he said, "Now we'll go."

We stepped into the orange glare and a soft, glittering rain. Patrick zipped the tent's fly behind us and we walked across the grounds and right through the open gateway, passing without a challenge between two gunnery emplacements, five soldiers on each, in their helmets and night goggles and armor. The gate rolled shut behind us and we entered the dark.

The rain let up, but still we had no moon. For thirty minutes we walked along the road without flashlights, going north, feeling with our feet for the ruts and the boggy soft spots. We didn't talk. The din of the reptiles and insects, our steps and our breaths, that's all we heard.

Headlights came up on the road far behind us. Shortly afterward, we heard the engine.

We stepped to the side, and the headlights stopped fifty feet short of us, and Patrick went to the vehicle, a Humvee, I thought, but I couldn't really see, and in a minute his silhouette came toward me and then disappeared as the car turned around and accelerated back the way it had come.

Now Roux directed our steps with a small flashlight. I could make out a sizeable package dangling from his arm. He slung it over his shoulder. As we walked it gave out a kind of clicking and muttering.

For quite a while the vehicle's aura remained visible behind us. I would have expected them to run blackout headlights, but they didn't seem to care.

When they were well away, Roux said, "We'll get off the road here, and take a rest."

"Let's not drown in a mudhole."

"No, it's good ground."

He found a spot he liked, laid out a handkerchief, and sat with his back to a tree. Between his knees he set down the package, a canvas haversack. He unbelted the flap, and I knelt beside him while he unpacked the contents by the beam of his penlight—it showed eerily on his eyeglass lenses, like two sparks in his face.

On top, a large manila envelope, inside it a map of the Democratic Republic of Congo. And cash. US twenties. "This is my money."

"Your funds when you arrived. It's all there."

No wallet, no cards of any kind. "Where's my passport?"

"You don't need it."

Also, a manila folder—the one I'd seen on the desk of the man from USSOCOM—holding, as far as I could tell in the dark, printed copies of my e-mails, as well as my handwritten pages, and not copies, but the originals themselves. "They're dusting their hands of me completely, aren't they? I bet they're burning my pajamas too."

Roux made no answer while I looked at some items wrapped in a hand towel. A metal fork and a spoon. A folding knife with a single blade. A penlight. "But what about a cell phone? How will I stay in contact?"

"They'll be able to locate you."

"Of course they will."

At the bottom of the sack rested two one-liter bottles of water, and at the very bottom, a cloth bag. Roux set the bag on the ground and opened it and trained his light on a lot of metallic lozenges, each wrapped in tissue paper.

I held my light in my teeth and unwrapped one. Considering its heft, it was small. Three fingers would have covered it.

A kilo of gold.

I said, "Goddamn! Goddamn!" and the light dropped from my mouth.

"Captain Nair, listen to me. In the first place, these are only twenty kilos."

"That's still a million dollars' worth. Goddamn!"

"Stop saying Goddamn." Roux set down his penlight and paused to polish his glasses on his shirttail. Squatting over my pile of riches. "In the second place, these are not genuine."

"Well, then, fuck. Fuck and Goddamn. Not genuine?"

He unwrapped another, shone his light on it, turning it in his dirty fingers. "The plating is copper and nickel, with some gold. Inside it's only lead."

"Who's going to fall for crap like this?"

"Nobody. It works only with complete amateurs—you know, drunken tourists lured in by pimps, that kind of thing. It's not for serious ruses, it won't pass any kind of knowledgeable inspection. It's something you can flash, nothing more. It's just for you to flash."

"This is outrageous."

Roux laughed and said, "I laugh because you're entertaining. I'm going back now." He scooped up the contents and fastened them inside the pack and stood up. He seemed in a rush. "Yours to carry."

I donned the pack. The load was heavy, but it was good equipment. Thick straps. I could probably hike a long way without chafing my armpits.

Facing him I understood, only now, that he was perhaps as tall as I. But he had a tininess of personality, and a sparrow's face, also tiny. So then even his size was an illusion. His Frenchness, his bag of gold, his lost wife—all fake.

"I'm instructed to tell you to get physically close to certain parties, keeping this material with you."

"That was my understanding."

"They'll maintain a fix on your location at all times. Remember that."

"Is this a drone operation?"

"I'm not aware of such a thing."

"Sure."

"I'm only a messenger, but I can assure you personally you won't be harmed. We don't fight like that, harming our own people."

"Sure. Except when you do."

He said, "Don't worry. Never worry. And don't drop your mission."

"I wouldn't consider it."

"If you do," Roux said, "if you drop out of contact—you'll be in an unacceptable situation. A kind of hell. Always hunted. Never resting. Nobody who tries it can last very long. You know it, don't you? Nobody ever lasts."

•

The US Army kept their garrison well out of the way. I had the road entirely to myself. By the fragrance, I guessed it cut through a forest of eucalyptus. The sack's contents clicked rhythmically and with every step I said yes, finally, yes, at last: I'm done with you all, done with your world, done with you all, done with your world.

Twenty kilos of nonsense on my shoulders. How many pounds? Better than forty. More like forty-five. How many stone? Something like three. Right around seven hundred ounces. Yet the pack felt weightless, until my giant excitement gave way to the question why I wasn't getting rid of it. Some item among the contents called out uninterruptedly to a global positioning satellite, a chopper full of Special Ops, a Predator drone, a fleet of drones—called out, after all, to the people who would either bring order to my affairs in a prison or murder me and solve my life.

I trudged for five hours, covering in that interval only a few miles. The dawn had begun—as always this near the equator very gradually, and even doubtfully—before I spied any huts among the trees.

I reached a slick soft spot I couldn't skirt unless I ranged far into the wood. I sidled left along its edge and came to a sucking, lethal-looking red-and-yellow mudhole sprouting dead limbs around its border. In such a pit anything might be drowned. I shrugged off the pack and opened it at my feet. I set aside my papers and cash, and the map, and the water. I gripped one strap and spun myself to get the pack whirling and let it fly ten meters. It slapped the surface, skidded, rolled slowly under.

My Timex said it was 6:17 on the twenty-sixth of October. Five days, nine hours left in which to find my way to Freetown. Plus an hour I'd pick up changing time zones. I unstrapped the watch from my wrist and pitched it underhanded into the muck.

Five thousand kilometers. One hundred thirty hours.

I drank down a liter of water as I stood there, tossed the bottle, kept the other, which wouldn't stay with me much longer. While the pack sank with anything metal—penlight, camp knife, phony kilos, the lot—I removed my shirt and used it as a bindle for the rest. I thought about tossing away my belt with its suspicious metal buckle, considered also the buttons on my shirt and trousers, realized I might as well go naked—what certainty would it bring? There's always something more to be rid of. Something inside.

•

I wondered about Michael. I expected him to turn up at my side having lingered in the area all this time, watching for some sign of me or of Davidia. As soon as I thought of him, there he was, Michael, crouched at the base of one of these tall trees just ahead—but it wasn't Michael. Only a termite berm. As the day came on it revealed many more such berms feeding on the eucalyptus, and I thought I saw blurry figures or ghosts crouched in the grove, watching me, and soon the woods were full, indeed, of people moving among the trees and poking slender sticks into the mounds, harvesting the white ants. I was joined on the way now by dozens of mud-spattered, stately women balancing baskets on their heads, taking the insects to the market. None of them spoke. They had the manner of ghosts. Possibly one of them had sprung from the corpse of the woman we'd struck down in Uganda. But their feet padded on the clay. I heard them breathing.

I followed them out of the woods and into Darba, a town

without electric light, without even useless wires, just old power poles broken at the tops like huge dead stalks. The place materialized around us in a haze of cook-smoke, a city of sturdy French colonial buildings without panes in the windows or doors in the doorways, concrete husks into which people had moved their animals while they made shanties of twig and adobe for themselves in the yards.

I stopped at a café, really a tent. I gave the barman a twenty-dollar bill and he left me sleeping on my face at his only table while his small daughter looked after the establishment.

I woke when a guy came in flying on what looked like the greatest drug ever made. He was speaking in tongues, his feet didn't touch the floor, he was just being lugged around by his smile; it turned out he was merely drunk on a few baggies' worth of "spirits" branded, in this case, as Elephant Train.

I bought him another and another, and as many for myself. When I asked him if he spoke English, he said, "Super English."

"Where is Newada Mountain?"

"You need to go La Dolce."

"How do I find La Dolce?"

"Go to Newada Mountain."

"No. No. Ou est La Dolce?"

"La Dolce!" I heard the two Italian words, though he might have said Ladoolchee.

"Is La Dolce near Newada Mountain?"

"She is the mother of Newada Mountain."

"A person? A woman? Une personne? Une femme?"

"Yes. The mother. Oui. La mère. Oui."

Elephant Train. I spread out my Congo map, and together we searched for Newada Mountain as we bit into many packets and sucked down the contents, but the map got smaller and Congo grew larger, and soon we were lost.

The barman returned and presented me with a pair of slip-on jogging shoes, blue in color, a pair of black denims called El Gaucho, and a yellow T-shirt with a woman's brown face on it. Who is the woman? I said, and he said, Très jolie! I said, Oui oui. He gave me my change in Ugandan shillings. I said, No Congo francs? and he said, Le franc?—c'est merde.

When I asked about Newada Mountain he said, It's there, pointing north, but I don't know how to get there. Go to the coffin maker. He's going to Newada. He's next to the church.

Yes, I see the church.

He's going to Newada Mountain. Follow the coffin maker.

The clock on the post stretched its hands out sideways, nine-fifteen. I'd walked for five hours, slept for one. Spent another getting drunk. Out back of the café I found a dry spot of earth to stand on among the puddles, and got myself into the new wardrobe. The jeans and T-shirt sagged quite a lot; the blue shoes fit perfectly over my grimy socks.

•

Behind the Église du Christ I found a man, a very small one, perhaps of the Mbuti, one of the Pygmy groups, dressed in a sports shirt and clean trousers and shiny plastic sandals. He stood with his hands on a green bicycle, rolling it backward and forward as if to check its worthiness. I said, "Are you the coffin maker?" He didn't understand. I tried to remember the French word for coffin but I never knew it in the first place. Somebody called to him, he abandoned me for a fool, and I followed him as he walked his bike along the crumbling tarmac street.

On sawhorses out front of his lean-to rested five bright purple coffins, two of them, I'm afraid, quite short. These were the two he was concerned with. He parked his bike's rear tire on a notched block to steady it and mounted both coffins—equal in length, about a meter—sideways behind the seat and fastened them down with black rubber straps, which he tightened and yanked and tightened again.

He high-stepped over the bar of his conveyance and straddled it while he rolled it free of the block and set his feet on the pedals. For a moment he stood in the air, then descended as he produced a forward motion. He knew I was watching. I don't think he liked it.

I followed some distance behind him, out of the town and into a small rain, then under a hot blue sky. The tarmac ended in a fog of red dust out of which the vast faces of speeding lorries exploded one after another, saying I AM LOST—TOUT AU BOUT—REGRETTE RIEN—coming within half an inch of touching us, as if some superstition required it. I lost him in the choking clouds until he left the highway for a sidetrack, and I glimpsed a bit of purple a quarter mile off to my right.

For some time I floated along like a marionette. I had no reason for believing these two small coffins were headed for Newada Mountain. We had the sun traveling toward our left, and therefore, it seemed, this track took us north, and north felt reason enough to be doing anything—that is, some particle of my memory put Newada to the north of where I'd first entered Congo with Michael and Davidia.

I had no problem keeping up, as he stopped often to get his strength. On the upward slopes he got off and walked his bike, and I pulled ahead of him. I never said hello or the like. My shoes held up, though my socks were falling to pieces. No blisters. The bottoms of my heels felt raw, but only slightly.

About three hours along, many kilometers from the highway, the green bike's rear tire went flat—perhaps owing to some sabotage, as the puncture happened in front of an establishment consisting of a bench and a bicycle pump, open for business, which business was tire repair. The repairman pried the tire loose from its rim, pulled out the inner tube, and went about patching it with a remnant cut from another inner tube.

While this went on I had the sense to find a kiosk and buy a bag of breadrolls and some candles and matches and two liters of water and a yellow number-two pencil and a small kitchen knife wrapped, for safety's sake, in newspaper. I paid with a five-thousand-shilling bill, and the proprietor and his wife shuttered their store and went to canvass their neighbors for the balance. They hadn't returned before the coffin maker set out again.

As far as I know, during the rest of the journey, as much as fifteen kilometers, I believe, the bearer of the coffins took no water. I ate my bread and drank down my two liters and then started dying of the drunkard's thirst.

I let him blaze the trail into another spell of rain and out again. We entered open farmland. In the mud, the treadprints of goats and barefoot humans. The wet fields shone hard enough to burn my eyes. We passed boys as they stopped hoeing to throw themselves down in the corn rows with their arms flung wide and their chins in the dirt, praying toward Mecca, but they sounded like coyotes howling. Just afterward, the coffins disappeared over a rise, and when I'd climbed to the top I looked across a landscape of rolling hills and silhouettes—the lumps of huts, a few skeletal, solitary trees, and three cell phone towers with much the same lonely and distinguished aspect, one in the north, two others beyond it in the northwest.

The coffin maker, already free of his cargo, charged back down the way he'd come. I moved to block his way. He skidded to a stop and leaned on his handlebars, tipping his bike to the side with one short leg outstretched and a toe on the ground, and when I asked him if this was Newada Mountain, he spoke his first words to me, saying, "Oui, c'est Newada," and kicked off again, gaining speed down the hill, and I gathered he'd reach the wider road before full dark. A bit along in his descent he turned his head and spoke once more, calling, "—le lieu du mal!" which I think means the bad or the wrong or the evil place.

•

ATTENDEZ EN ANGLAIS:
FINDER PLEASE DELIVER THIS MATERIAL TO
THE UNITED STATES MILITARY GARRISON
NEAR DARBA, CONGO

TO WHOM IT MAY CONCERN (US MILITARY PERSONNEL):
PLEASE FORWARD ATTACHED MATERIAL TO

DAVIDIA ST. CLAIRE
C/O GARRISON CMDR COL. MARCUS ST. CLAIRE
US 10TH SPEC FORCES, FT. CARSON, COLORADO, USA

WITH GRATITUDE—KAPTAJN ROLAND NAIR (CAPT.)
JYDSKE DRAGONREGIMENT, HRN (ROYAL DANISH ARMY)

[OCT 27 ca. 12AM]

Davidia,

I wish I could record this silence. It's like the bottom of the sea. In silence like this, my head makes its own noise—I can hear the moon, I can hear the stars. Once in a while a sick child croaks in one of the huts.

(I started to write this a couple of hours ago. I lit a candle, but the flame drew the nocturnal insects, including a moth big as a sparrow that batted out the flame in its forays and then crashed at my feet with its paraffin-spattered wings on fire and lay there flailing and burning for several minutes—all because of its infatuation . . . And then I saw the half moon coming up, so I've waited for its light to write by, sitting in the doorway of this hut. I'm guessing as to time of day, but the moon's been waxing fatter and rising later and I remember it rose around ten pm when last I owned a watch.)

I won't bother catching you up. Someday I'll attach this to a full account. I'll wrap it all in brown paper and tie it with string and plunk it in a DHL pouch addressed to you, or to Tina Huntington. Which of you am I writing to?

To you, Davidia. Just letting you know (should only this fragment reach you) that as of the date above, I was still alive.

For the third time in ten days, I'm a captive—not held by others, but stuck, no option for movement. In my universe, time and space converge on 3 pm Nov 2nd at the Bawarchi Restaurant in Freetown—remember the Bawarchi?—5000 kilometers and 112 hours from here and now. Not a clue how to get there.

I have some candles and matches, but as I say—the crashing bugs. I've got paper and pencils and a knife. The clothes on my back. 720 US dollars. 60K Ugandan shillings. No credit cards or plane tickets, no passport, no documented actuality. No pills against malaria. Every day, more African.

I think when the wind shifts I may be hearing the brook at the bottom of the hill, or people down there laughing, or weeping.

Several hours ago, Davidia, at dusk, I climbed this hill and arrived at the village of New Water Mountain. I stood among a couple dozen huts. No mountain visible. Hooves and feet had beaten the hilltop's ground into a flat, muddy waste. The only splashes of color came from yellow twenty-liter water jugs—they lay all around. And two bright, child-size purple coffins. Beside the coffins, two old men scraped at the ground, one with a hoe, one with a spade, both men barefoot but wearing long sleeves and trousers.

Nearby, a man and a woman seemed to be taking apart

one of the dwellings, removing its thatch, setting the materials aside. The woman stopped, laid her head back, and put her face to the sky—I expected a mournful howl, but she only trembled a bit, then settled her mind, it seemed, and returned to the work.

A giant leafless tree, an arthritic-looking horror, dominates the vicinity from the top of the rise (I can hear it creaking in the breeze right now as I write). Four people stood at the tree's base, hallooing up toward the highest branches like hounds. One of them, a white woman, met me as I approached, and she said, "Are you wondering where the chickens went?"—I said I wasn't—"And the goats? They're all dead. And most of the children. Dead. Are you lost?"—I said a little—"You look disturbed."—She meant drunk. I said I was.

She'd walked among several villages with these others, two women and a sturdy-looking man with a machete on his shoulder, all Africans. She alone was white—white and plump, probably in her thirties—and grimy from hiking, but hale and upright.

I said, "Jesus, I know you."

"You know Jesus?"

"I saw you at the White Nile Hotel, didn't I? You were swimming in the pool."

"My husband Jim and I are from the North East Congo Mission of the Seventh-day Adventist Church."

"I had the impression it was something like that."

"It's the Lord's work," she said, "but every day you want to kill somebody."

The man with the machete said, "We must go, Mom."

"I know. I just said so."

She told me her husband had spent the day in Darba trying to find someone from the Ministry of Health so they could get some action up here. "Or the Red Cross or somebody. What a laugh. But we have to try."

"What about Doctors Without Borders?"

"He'll check with them too, but they like to stay close to Bunia for supplies. Close to the airfield. And the brothels. We call them Doctors Without Pants."

The woman continually waved her hands and flicked her fingers as if battling with cobwebs, and I feared for her sanity as much as mine. She said, "We've looked at three other villages in the last two days. It's the same thing for fifty kilometers around. The people are crazy, the water is poison, everybody's dying. We've convinced them to evacuate—all but this bunch. They've got a queen who rules them from the treetop. Come over here and you can look."

We joined the others. Several meters above us, between two large boughs, a chair was hanging. We could see the bottom of the chair, and a pair of feet, in white tennis shoes, dangling below it, and in the boughs above the chair were bunches of thatch, evidently to protect the owner of the feet.

"She won't come down till morning, but we can't wait for that. We're meeting the reverend in Kananga. It's two kilometers down that path. Or more."

The feet up above seemed quite still. "Is she asleep?"

"I don't know what she is. Are you gold, or hydrocarbons?"

"Pardon?"

"Are you with one of the companies? Which particular corporation?"

"None. I'm here looking for a friend of mine, but I haven't spotted him. Or much of anybody, actually."

We stood on a patch of brown earth littered with corn husks and cassava peelings. To the west I saw a couple of distant cell towers, lone trees, many huts—all in two dimensions, flat against the sunset. In the other direction, everything was bathed in a somber metallic light, and the two child coffins, ten steps away, seemed uniquely purple, a purple without precedent. Beside them, the two old diggers had nearly disappeared into the earth. I went over and looked. The margin between the twin graves had crumbled to make a single large hole. As they smoothed its sides with their tools, the men sloshed up to their ankles in muddy seepage, maybe the very stuff that had killed the poor tots.

She said, "Usually when somebody dies they do a big wake with a lot of howling and drumming, but they've had too many, and now it's just a chore. The whole region is toxic, thanks to the lust for precious metals. This is the outworking of a spiritual travesty. Are you any kind of believer?"

"No."

"We're getting out of here day after tomorrow, and I am Goddamn glad."

"How are you traveling?"

"Walking, for now. Jim has the Trooper. We'll make one more swing through the villages, and then back to Lubumbashi. We'll take a plane from Bunia."

"Look," I said, "if I find my friend, we'll need a ride out of here. I don't mind paying, and I don't mind begging."

"It depends on how many come in the car. Where are you going?"—I said I didn't know—"Any decent hotel, am

I right?"—I said yes—she recommended Bunia. "There's quite a bit of UN activity there. Peacekeepers and such. It's a UN town."

"How far away is Bunia?"

"A couple hundred kilometers. It's the nearest airstrip. The UN uses it, and some charters."

"Please, ma'am. Please. We don't need seats. Put us on the roof. Really. This is Africa."

She thrilled me by saying, "We'll probably come right through here day after tomorrow. We'll do our best to take you aboard. Look for a blue Isuzu Trooper with the top painted white."

"I'll be looking for it, believe me."

"In the meantime, you'll meet the queen. Maybe they'll elect you king."

"Are you laughing at me?"

"After a while," she said, "everything's funny." For one second—I think because of her bright anger—she seemed sexy. She turned to her friends. "Next is Kananga. Only a couple of miles, yes?"

They walked on, four abreast. I watched them get away. Toward the bottom of the hill a flashlight came on, and its spot trembled over the ground . . . I hadn't learned the woman's name or told her mine or even asked if she'd seen anybody like Michael.

The sun had set. The West turned a densely luminous terrifying aubergine. I stood alone beside the queen's tree. I tried shouting Michael's name and got no answer. As far as I could tell, the queen slept on undisturbed.

I looked into one or two huts. The people inside them ignored me, even when I called to them.

Then the night came down, and I found this hut empty and came in and sat inside, right here on the dirt floor, and this is where I've lived for the last few hours—maybe till I die—probably of thirst. I haven't had water since noon. Soon I'll go down and drink from the toxic creek.

[OCT 27 ca. 7AM]

When a woman's screaming disturbed my dreams I thought nothing of it—there's always some woman or infant or animal screaming—and I stayed under the darkness in my head as long as possible before I woke up thirsty and frightened in this hut. I'm crouched in a corner. The female screams go on. A sound of hammering or chopping too—not rhythmic, just violent. I have to piss. I need water. A man screams also.

This thirst is murdering me. Give me sewage—I'll drink it. But I can't look for the creek now. I'm afraid to leave this hut.

Davidia. I've had a look. It's Michael out there. Adriko. Our Michael.

I'm not going out. I'm glad to see him—I came here looking for him—but I won't make myself known until I have an idea what's happening.

I see a lot of villagers sitting on the ground around the coffins and the grave and the dirt piles. Michael argues—battles—with a large woman. He and this screamer are the only ones standing, stalking one another in a circle ten meters wide, keeping the people and the coffins and the double grave between them.

I'm able to count twenty-nine sitting on the ground. Women wearing long skirts and tops with bold patterns and colors, men in sweaters or large T-shirts with washed-out logos, all of them looking as if they'd rolled in the mud and didn't care. Two women with children laid across their laps. Both kids naked and bony and sick, eyes open and staring at another world. One woman in a brilliant but filthy wrap and headscarf sits on top of a dirt pile, her legs out straight.

Michael holds a machete two-handed. Sometimes he raises it above his head as if he means to chop the sun out of the sky. He and the woman scream in some kind of Creole or Lugbara unintelligible to me.

My guess: the woman is the village queen, La Dolce, down from her tree—I recognize her tennis shoes—and these people have gathered for the funeral of the two dead children, and Michael must have stopped it with his screams and his machete. He and La Dolce howl at each other to the point of strangling on their hatred, but not both at once—it's back and forth—that is, it seems to proceed as a debate while they orbit around the others.

She wears a long black skirt and a man's sleeveless undershirt torn off just below her breasts, which, by their outlines, are narrow and pendulous.

She's got a buzz-cut Afro on her hippopotamus head, eyes leaping from the sockets and eyelids like birds' beaks closing over them—her mouth is tiny and round, but it opens to shocking hugeness, displaying many square white teeth. A broad nose like a triangle biscuit smashed onto her face. She's fat and laughing, hips banging as she struts around, keeping the people and the coffins and the grave between her and Michael.

The hair on Michael's head is growing back. He tromps around in rubber sandals, blue jeans, a gray hooded sweatshirt, waving the machete with his left hand, slapping his right hand against his chest, where it says HARVARD.

Mainly throughout all this I feel thirsty. I've had nothing to drink since yesterday afternoon, and all this drama—and the whole sky, and the earth—and the oceans—seem tiny beside my thirst.

One minute ago Michael started chopping away with his machete at the woman's chair, which rests on the ground beside her tree, and she shimmied toward him majestically and plopped herself right down in it, daring him to keep up the destruction and split her in pieces as well.

He's speaking English—"I'll destroy this place!"

Now she doesn't howl, but rather sings of her power, I think, sitting on her throne, and cries out I think Bring me food! Bring me food! until a woman delivers something on a plastic plate and backs away apologizing. La Dolce flings grain into her mouth, it spills all over her bare belly, which even from here I can see is covered with stretch marks. Water now! Bring me water! They hurry to bring her a liter of bottled water—bottled Goddamn water. She anoints her own head from it and sprinkles her face. The drops remain while she says to Michael in English:

"I am El Olam—the Everlasting God!"

They've stopped everything. He's catching his breath. Listen, Davidia—his face frightens me. The blade is twitching in his hands.

She laughs at him.

I need water and I'm going out now before Michael kills her.

[OCT 27 ca. 5:30PM]

The sun is low and very red and mean. I can't look west.

Down to double digits: 94 hours to go. Plus 30 minutes. Still 5000 KM to cover.

I've drunk my fill at the creek. No matter. The toxins work slowly. Thirst would have killed me by tomorrow. I'm resting beside the creek among some new associates, that is, four skeletal sad-eyed Brahma cattle and the three herdsmen who tend them. Later I'll tell you all about these guys.

I don't intend to move from this haven, I'm at my leisure to write and also to drink, and not just water, and I'll tell you all about that too, but first—as to this morning's romp—

When I came out of my hiding-hut, Michael was declaring again:

"I'll destroy this place!" With a sweep of his machete he said, "You people are crazy!"

I stood by my doorway till Michael noticed. At first he didn't, but the villagers watched me. Without the usual smiling and laughing, their mouths took up no room in their faces and their eyes seemed abnormally huge.

The sight of me slapped Michael awake. His recognition of me seemed to travel up from his feet and when it got to his face I came closer, but not in reach of the machete.

He looked around himself: a dozen or so huts; the one tree—deceased; two piles of red dirt; two purple coffins, and a hole; also his clansmen huddling together on the ground like survivors of a shipwreck.

He said: "Where is she?" He meant you, Davidia.

"The Americans had us," I said. "Your outfit, the Tenth."

"Where is she, Nair?"

"She's gone. She got on a chopper and didn't look back."

His spine withered. The weapon dangled at his side. "Sometime during Arua, she took her heart away from me. I felt it. In Arua, something happened."

I wanted to take him away from this scene and talk about that other scene, about you, Davidia, and the colonel and the prop-wash and the noisy cloud that ate you up.

However: the Dolce woman strode up to my face and gave out a hearty, phony laugh and cried, "God knocked backwards!"

Michael said, "This woman is insane."

I said, "You must be La Dolce."

She yelped, "You've got an English for us!!??" (I punctuate excessively because her manner came straight out of comic books. She communicated in yelps, whoops—what else—guffaws, huzzahs, preachments, manifestos—and I had to agree instantly with Michael that she was insane.) "You are right, because I am!!!—I AM LA DOLCE!!!"

"What a stupid name to call yourself," Michael said.

She raised her face to Heaven and sang ha-hah.

"I understand she's the village queen or something."

"More than that. She's a priestess of genocide."

La Dolce addressed her brethren, pointing at Michael's head. "Do you hear the Devil talking in his mouth?"

"She calls me her prisoner," Michael said. "She tells them I'm being kept here by her power."

"She speaks good English."

"She's from Uganda. She's the cousin of my uncle."

La Dolce pointed at me now, almost touching my nose: "This one's clan is called Bong-ko. Their lies make you laugh!!!"

Michael said, "They know the truth about you." I said What?—he said, "Aren't you a liar? Why are you here without Davidia? If the Tenth got hold of you, how did you get away? Did you sell me for your freedom? How long before they come for me?" He raised high the machete. "I feel like cutting the lies right out of you!"

The blade didn't scare me so much—only the look of him. His beard was growing out in streaks and whorls. Nappy head, red eyes, fat parched lips. He'd plastered the laceration on his forearm with red mud. His greasy black face, his mangled sweatshirt, his mistreated jeans—all dabbed and smeared with it. His sandals and feet were tainted with the same African muck.

"Michael. Lower your weapon. I need water."

"I can't help you. Do you see her crazy eyes?" La Dolce sat in her wooden chair like an enormous toddler, broadcasting happy rage. "This woman is calling for a sacrifice. She wants to bury someone alive. If I don't keep an eye on her, she'll throw one of these people into the grave."

"Has she got more bottled water?"

"She's got a whole commissary."

"Where?—Please."

"Die of thirst, Nair. You sold me to the machine."

"I've got no time for your accusations."

"You should be the one to go in the grave with those children."

"Lower your weapon and help your friend."

"Sacrifice for sacrifice."

"Two things," I said, backing away. "First, water. And then we get out of here." I guess I looked stupid, stumbling off. And he looked stupid with his cutlass in the air, as if it was stuck there and he couldn't get it down.

I poked my head into several huts and found one stacked with half a dozen cases of bottled water and boxes of cereal and canned goods, its entrance guarded by a man leaning on a hoe. He took it up like a cudgel when I got near. I tried to bribe him with all my Ugandan shillings, then with US dollars—twenty, a hundred, two hundred—but he wouldn't share.

I experienced a sort of dislocation here. The next several minutes have gotten away from me, and I'm not sure I remember things in their actual order.

I saw the villagers all standing around the grave, shuffling their feet in place as they moaned and trembled. They were dancing. Singing.

La Dolce and Michael had resumed their own dance, circling the scene.

I didn't notice that the purple coffins had gone until they reappeared on the shoulders of four men coming two-by-two from behind me. The dead children, I assumed, traveled inside them. The crowd made way, still chanting and moving in a zombie trance.

The diggers waited in their hole and each coffin was just shoved over into their double embrace and let down to the floor with a little sploosh, and then helping hands raised one of the men from his work, while the other simply stepped onto one of the coffins and clambered out on his own, leaving behind the smeary impression of his bare foot.

La Dolce screamed at some length, and Michael spoke briefly in a much lower tone, both in Lugbara, I supposed.

The mob circled the grave on their knees, shoving dirt into it with their hands. They tossed the piles back into the holes and then bowed their heads while their queen made a speech that included much repetition of "La Dolce, La Dolce." When she got near me, she took up her theme in English: "What is that name? I am La Dolce Vita!! You know it means that life is sweet. That's me. I bring life. Life is sweet. But first we must sacrifice. First God will take what he wants. He takes the babies into his jaws. Can we stop him?" She went among the crowd, looking into face after face, bending close: "Can you stop God?—Can you stop God? What about you?—Can you stop God? No!! You cannot!!! And now God is angry that you have not sacrificed. I know this because I am God!" I doubt they comprehended.

Michael said to her, "The Newada people are not animists and sacrificers like that. This village used to be Christian"—he pronounced it Chrishen. Then he shouted, still in English:

"Go home! The grave is full enough! Go home!"

Many of the mob stood up and wandered away. Some of them wept, nobody talked. A dozen or so stayed with their queen.

La Dolce watched the others go, and I got the sense that Michael had triumphed here.

The queen performed a kind of slow elephantine dance, singing ha-hah, ha-hah. She pointed at Michael's crotch and said, "I'm going to my sleep now. When I dream, your parts will turn into a white stone!"

Michael laughed. It was false, but loud, from deep in his lungs. He said, "Woman! If I had diesel, I would soak you and burn you alive."

"La Dolce is going up!" The queen lowered her butt into her throne with an ostentatious lot of wiggling. The two diggers hurried to help her.

Next to the tree stood a rough-hewn table with some items on it—a few liters of bottled water—empty—a whole cassava, some mangoes, and some of the green oranges they eat in this region. From nails hammered into the trunk hung plastic shopping bags by their knots, full of what I don't know. Clothes, probably, food. A pole jutted from the earth nearby, and between it and the tree some bright things flapped on a length of twine—a scarf, a skirt, a T-shirt. A pair of white athletic socks. Stair treads had been hacked in a zigzag up the trunk, but La Dolce didn't use them.

La Dolce raised one finger and made a winding motion with it and two stout women and a man took hold of her rope. She laughed and laughed while, by a system of pulleys anchored out of sight above, they hoisted her chair off the ground, and she ascended into the boughs.

We tilted back our heads to watch—the chair swaying, the rope rasping against the tree's rough hide, the crowd's murmurs and exclamations—ayeee ayeee—the wind coming across the expanse.

She pointed down at Michael. "Hees name shall rot!"

I remembered a spider I'd seen swinging in just such a manner from Michael Adriko's toothbrush. I thought: Yes, everything's coming together now.

I wouldn't have thought that anything could distract me from my thirst, but now I heard the sound of an engine, and a burst of hope lifted me. "Is that a car?"

It was a cow. Another one also moaned.

I said, "Shit. We can't ride out of here on cattle."

Michael took a couple of strokes at the tree with his machete. He gave it up and seemed about to walk off somewhere.

"Michael—I need you to focus now. I talked to some missionaries. Tomorrow they can take us out of here to Bunia."

"Good for them."

"Don't do this. Jesus, man—not now. I need to get to Freetown, and I'm out of ideas."

"Leave me alone."

"I need your help."

"Leave me alone."

When he's like that, he's like that. I left him alone.

I followed the path down the hill.

While a humpbacked Brahma cow was loosing a stream of piss two meters away, I sponged up creek water in a dirty sock and squeezed it into my mouth. No liquid so sweet has ever touched my lips, until perhaps five minutes later—because gathered around a stump quite near to where I'd fallen on my knees, three remnant herdsmen had convened. One of them offered me a gourd. I thought he meant it for a water glass, but in fact it was already swimming with a filmy yellow liquid, pungently alcoholic, and I knew I'd come among my tribe.

Three fine men: one younger, two older. I forget their names. They have the puffy look of corpses floating in formalin. And three stunted, starving cows and one bull who drags his chin across the ground because he can't hold up his own horns.

As far as I make out through the language barrier, they've been trading off the last of their cattle for plantain and sugar cane, which they bury together in a formula that ferments and emerges as a remarkable beverage they call Mawa. I don't think it's good for the teeth—they've got none. But these dregs in the gourd, I'll bet you, give strength to the bones.

I can't say whether they're from Michael's clan or some

neighboring society. They wear rope sandals. Long-sleeved shifts of coarse cloth, brown or gray, depending on the light.

I fell asleep by the creek, I woke from a long nap, and I've been sitting here writing away with no intention of leaving this spot because, if I take their meaning, a new batch of Mawa comes up from the earth around sundown, and I plan to be here for the resurrection. Prior to my nap, I only got a few swallows.

I'm not going back up that hill to deal with Michael. I'd sooner take my chances on the Tenth Spec Forces than hang my hopes on Michael Adriko, the lunatic comedian.

I should stay sober and alert for the sound of a blue-and-white Isuzu.

Really? Kiss off. What difference does it make? It's been two weeks since we left Arua and I've come altogether about fifty kilometers.

[SAME-SAME, 6:30PM?]

Oh, Davidia! Or maybe I mean

Oh, Tina!

Whichever is your name, I call to you, oh woman of my heart.

The Mawa decants out of 2 five-liter jugs.

The gourd bowl goes round and round.

My flat black silhouette comrades. Right now they stand against the sunset. Behind them it looks like Dresden's burning. I forget their names. I'll ask again.

—Oudry

—Geslin

—Armand

Priests of the nectar, ministers to the flock, of whom I am one.

If I can't buy or think my way out of this by tomorrow, I'll go back to the Americans and say, Prison? Fine.

My handwriting may be illegible—let's blame the dark.

Also my pencil must be dull, but come on, enough—it worries the mind and body to have to sharpen a utensil every half page.

Oudry, Geslin, and Armand have kindled a fire from dried dung on a bed of former thatch, and our laughter flies up into the blackness with its sparks.

Incidentally, Davidia, that's why they're tearing the huts apart around here. For firewood.

Davidia, I wish you could meet Tina.

Tina, I'm not sure I'd like you to meet Davidia.

Do I contradict myself? Not to worry. I'll soon be transcribing these notes in a prison cell, with plenty of time to get my thoughts in order.

Let's face it. I've got to go back to the Yanks.

I've improved the plan a bit: take the last of my cash to Bunia, lavish it on a finale of booze and prostitutes, then advise the UN to arrest me.

Fifty kilometers in 14 days. Per my calculations, a circus clown walking on his hands would have made better progress.

Tina.

You're sexy, Tina. And smart. But not glamorous in the Michael's-woman way. Still. You might have had dealings with Michael. I think you might have dealt with him. You know what I mean? I mean, did you fuck him, Tina? I always suspected you did but I never asked, so I'm asking. Did you fuck Michael?

[OCT 28 ca. 8AM]

When next I encountered Michael Adriko, I found him continuing in a wretched state. He looked like he'd been beaten about the face with a bat, but it was just sadness, only misery, it was nothing physical, it was all from the inside. That was last night.

A few words about remorse.

This remorse twists in me like seasickness.

If you've been seasick lately you know what I mean. This remorse is physically intolerable.

I climbed the hill last night after drinking with my fellow herdsmen. What are their names? God. I've lost their names—and the herdsmen as well, and their cattle. Where are they? I'm alone by the creek.

There's a reason they call them spirits. They enter in, they take control, they speak and walk around. Wicked, wicked spirits.

Last night I thought I heard Michael chopping with his machete atop this hill. Striking at La Dolce's tree and calling, Nair! with every stroke, Nair! Nair!

It must have been well past midnight, because the moon rode high and gave plenty of light to see by. I floated zigzag up the hill and now report I was hallucinating. Nobody was bothering the tree.

Michael sat against its base with his legs splayed before him and his machete sticking upright at the midpoint between his feet, his arms limp beside him, his chin on his chest—in Kandahar I once saw a man sitting exactly like that, and he was dead.

I said, "I don't care if you're awake, or dead, or what."

"I'm defeated, that's all."

"We need to go, man. What's keeping you here?"

"Something has to happen that hasn't happened."

"What could possibly happen?"

"Davidia might come."

"Davidia's not coming. She was disgusted right down through. She didn't look back, Michael. Not one glance."

"I put her to too harsh a test."

"Did you think you'd be the king here, and Davidia would reign beside you as queen?"

"You're making my experience sound shallow. You're wrong. This is cutting me very deep. I never meant to keep her here. No, I only meant to bring my wedding to these people as a great gift, and then leave. I always meant for us to leave."

"Leave how?"

"There's always a plan for extraction. How many times have I told you that?"

"What plan? Who extracts us?"

"In this case, we extract ourselves."

"Then let's do it. For God's sake, Michael."

"What are you made of, Nair? Why did you betray us?"

"Will you leave it for another time? Let's get out of here, if you know a way."

"I'm not leaving."

"Come and have some Mawa with these folks down the hill. Let's relax, and talk this over."

He wouldn't respond. I walked away in the hope he'd hop up and follow me, as a dog might.

The truth was that we'd finished the Mawa to the last molecule and sopped up all the dregs. For this reason, if I had an errand in walking away, I forgot it.

My feet turned me around, and I stood over Michael once again. "Very good, sir. What's happening?"

"You're drunk."

"Let's talk a little bit about betrayal."

"You're an expert."

"There's betrayal, and there's betrayal."

"So far I can't argue with you."

"I need your help."

"Go away."

"Gladly."

I repeated the same business—I had no control over my words or my deeds. The spirits possessed me. Down the hill became up the hill, and I'm back at him.

"Before I go, I just want to say goodbye to the biggest idiot I've ever known."

"Goodbye then. You won't get far."

"I'm resigned to that. Let the Yanks play with me awhile. I'm headed for prison."

"What do they care about you, really?"

"Do you think you're the only idiot with criminal secrets and idiotic criminal scenarios, who does idiotic things?"

"You're raving. If I had some rope, I'd tie you."

"I'm going to the bottom of the hill and start waiting for these missionaries. They've got a car."

"Excellent. Maybe you'll pass out, and they'll run you over."

The spirits carried me down the hill once more. Demons. Vandals. Fiends. This time a sense of calm overcame me, a desperate counterfeit sobriety in which I realized I'd better talk clearly and persuasively to this stupid asshole.

Michael was actually on his feet when I returned.

"Hey. Where are you going?"

"Don't follow me."

"I forgot what I wanted to say before. It's just this: there's some business in Freetown I need to conclude in something of a hurry."

"In a hurry? Where do you think you are?"

"I've negotiated the sale of some material," I said, "and the handoff's in Freetown with no fallback, and I'm afraid the deadline has gotten very tight. Thursday afternoon."

"What's got you so mad for it? Is there money in this?"

"Until the window closes. Can we get to Freetown?"

"There are UN flights out of Bunia."

"How can we get on a flight?"

"Money and luck."

"I think we'd better try. Otherwise I'm in a lot of trouble. Yesterday a fellow promised me hell."

"The promise was true."

"He meant I couldn't last on the run, I'll end up turning

myself in, and you're right about that much—the promise is true. What else can I do but give myself up? Help me."

"Not now. Go sleep it off."

"Goddamn it! You said you had a plan. Oh, well. I'd be a liar if I said I ever actually believed you—I'd be a liar."

"That's exactly what you are. A liar."

"Wait. I'm sorry. Wait."

"I said don't follow me."

I called him a cowardly little wog, and a black-ass nigger.

"Shall I knock you down?"

"I'll get up, you nigger. I'll get up, and I'll keep coming."

"You're trying to hurt me. And that hurts me."

And me. He was, after all, the only man in whose embrace I'd spent the night, more than once, on the cold desert ground outside Jalalabad one November, and in the strength of his arms I grew warm, I rested, I slept . . . I said, "Goddamn you for a fucking coon."

"Fine. Go ahead. That's fine."

"I know every word for you. My mother's people live in Georgia. They still fly the rebel flag over there."

"Fine, fine. You forget I spent time in North Carolina."

"Fort Bragg, that's right. Fort Carson. Every American fort there ever was."

"I've seen those Confederate flags."

In the orange moonlight he looked down at his feet, really examined them, lifting one and then the other, and it occurred to me I could get in a couple of good blows while he let this pointless business distract him, I could pretty well box his ears. I must have tried it, because I found myself with the breath knocked out of me and white streaks rocketing around the corners of my head. Sucking at a vacuum, it felt like.

"Aren't you going to get up? I heard you say you'd keep coming."

My mouth and nose were in the mud. The demons made no reply.

He knelt beside me and stuck his blade in the ground one millimeter from my ear. I thought he might finish me off quietly with a chokehold.

"This is why you never got promoted beyond your captain rank. Your childish temper."

[OCT 30 NOON]

Davidia, and Tina—

If this communication has come to you raw, before I've had a chance to transcribe these notes properly—or blend them with my someday semi-honest account—then you see the ink. No more pencils. You see my hand is sturdy. You're looking at a fresh page.

You guess my fortunes have turned. In which direction, I'll tell you in a minute. This much for now: I've had a meal or two, and a wash at a sink, and I'm wearing new clothes. Let me finish the story.

After the fight with Michael, I slept facedown on the ground.

In the morning, Michael woke me gently. He said, "How was the night?"

He seemed very different. He had a liter of delicious

bottled water for me to drink. As soon as its mouth touched mine, I drained it away.

The sky was gray through and through. The air seemed soft. Nothing stirred. I wondered if the clan had all died in the night, all of them at once.

When I was able to stand, Michael led me to a part of the creek where I could bathe in it up to my chest with my clothes on, African style. It looked like a genuine creek—a rapids and small falls—a place where folks might come to cool off and to draw good water; but the water was bad, and nobody came.

The clouds blew off and the morning sky turned blue. I came back to life and noticed some gaunt cows and even a couple of young goats pushing their noses around on the earth nearby. I lay out on a warm flat rock in the sunshine. Michael sat beside me, smoking—how, I'd like to know, does he produce cigarettes out of thin air?

At this point I noticed that my head ached and that I felt, all around, unhappy. Here's a confession: I'd puked while unconscious, and I'd lain all night facedown in my own sick. If I'd passed out while lying on my back I'd have drowned in it, and my labors would be done, but no such luck. Meanwhile Michael was saying:

"Life is short. But the time is long. I look back, I see so much, my childhood . . ."

While I lay in a woozy stew of crapulence—that is an actual word—Michael told me what he'd been doing since his escape from the Congolese Army: traveling without money, stumbling by the roadside, crawling through the fields like the Frankenstein beast. He spent two days camped near the US garrison, but couldn't form a plan. I couldn't help you, Michael said, I couldn't help Davidia, I couldn't help myself. There was nothing I could do. So I just came here—where again, there's nothing I can do. My people are sick, insane, they're burning their own huts, they don't have any food. Not one of them can remember me. They know the names of my mother and father, my mother's brother, my father's two cousins who owned a business selling cloth and rope—but they don't remember the children, not me, or my brother who died, or my two sisters who also died in the disturbances back then, when I left the clan. And poof, our existence is erased. And this woman, La Dolce. I'd like to kill her . . .

Michael went on to say:

"I believe I was nine years old the first time I killed someone. I'm not sure how old I was—I don't know how old I am now, really."

"Tell me it was a woman, or a child."

"What's the point of saying that?"

"I don't know. I think you're trying to be poignant, and I'm trying to undercut you."

"There were two of them, and I don't know who they were. It was during the reprisals. Our clan did nicely, you know, during the time of Idi Amin Dada, because he was Kakwa too. But when he ran away, the machetes came out against the Kakwa, and this creek ran with our blood. I returned here after the village was taken over . . . This is where it happened. I heard two people talking in a hut, only their voices, not the words, not even the kind of voice—man or woman or child—and I threw in a stick of dynamite. The hut was right over there. You walked through my first murders with your feet . . . Now I return once again, and everything is dead. Have I brought down a curse on my own clan? What have I done? Have I done something?"

I'd never known Michael to be afraid, not really. Certainly not terrified like this.

I lay there on my back, hanging on to my mind, or the equilibrium, let's say, of my essence—then no longer hanging on, realizing there's no point.

Michael said:

"And I was never with Tina. Even if I was with her before you came along, I would have told you."

"I believe you. I was crazy. And there's something I want to say as well. Are you listening?"

"I hear you."

I sat up and looked straight at him and tried hard to make him believe this—because it's true—"I'd never grass a friend. I might try and steal his girl and leave him to drown in shit while—well, while running off with his girl. But I'm not a snitch. Never."

Michael tossed his machete into the pool and it sank.

"Holy shit, man. We might need that."

"As God is my witness, and as long as I live, I shall never take another life. I shall never kill even one more person. I will die instead, if I have to."

He'd stubbed out his cigarette half-smoked and rested it on the rock beside him. Now he straightened it out, took a matchbox from his pants pocket, and spent a couple of minutes lighting it and smoking it down to the filter and looking satisfied with himself. He tossed the butt at the water and stood up, offering me a hand. "Now it's time to go. Where do we meet the missionaries?"

"At the road down the hill—the east side, where you come in."

"When do we meet them?"

"I don't even know if they're actually coming. But the lady said sometime today."

"Let's go and wait for them. We need to get to Bunia."

"Michael," I said, "you can make it here, but I can't. I'm no African. I'm like Davidia that way."

"So where do you think you're going?"

"I suppose it's prison."

"Do you think I'd let them put you in prison?"

"Is there any other way?"

"Haven't I told you from the beginning? There's always a plan for extraction." He made a sound like a pig at a trough—sucking back tears. His pride in himself, at this moment, had brought on a seizure of sentiment. "After everything, it's still the two of us."

Davidia: As we walked out of the village, the hippopotamus-woman La Dolce roused her clan and harried them after us partway down the hill. She cried, "Laugh at them, laugh at them!" and then "Riez! Riez!"

She said: "Don't touch them, don't talk to them, do you see the Devil in their eyes? Riez! Riez!"

I didn't think them capable of it, but one or two coughed up shreds of laughter and spit them at us. Soon the whole mob was yammering like dogs. Michael bowed his back. His head hung low. "Riez! Riez!" Like hens, like terrified geese. I followed behind him as he was driven from his family.

[NOV 1 6PM]

Dear Tina, Dear Davidia—

Again I'm writing to you by candlelight, but only because the power's blinked out in our corner of Freetown.

We're staying, now, at the National Pride Suites, which have nothing to be proud of. Out the window, West Africa: a lane like a sewer. Cockeyed shanties. Inexplicable laughter.

Downstairs there's a bar, intermittently air-conditioned, fragrant with liquor and lime and the cologne of prostitutes, but I'm not a patron—I'm on an indefinite drinks moratorium, thanks to a bargain I've made with Michael. And without the drinks, the women seem stripped of their appeal.

In any case, I'm not one hundred percent. Nursing a bit of a belly—that Goddamn Newada creek. Apparently certain microbes thrive on heavy metals.

However, the small percent of me that feels all right feels absolutely wonderful.

I don't need booze, or sex. I've spent the last two hours napping with my head on a sack full of cash. One hundred thousand US dollars. Minus recent expenses. Not a substantial cushion, just one thousand pieces of paper zipped up in a plastic carrier pouch, but oh how comfortable, and how sweet my dreams.

Tina, I hope you got out of Amsterdam. Hope you got away. Hope you didn't sit there waiting for the poisonous fallout from my ruin.

Hah. "Fallout."

But Tina, I'm serious: someday I'll put it all down in words and send it to you, and I'll enclose this last note on top. I don't know what a thorough confession might do for you, or what it might do to ease this combination of dread and anger working at my insides . . . For whatever it's worth, someday—the story from beginning to end.

And the end will be spectacular: Michael and I riding to Bunia in an Isuzu Trooper all heavenly blue and purified white packed with Seventh-day Adventists, and our intrepid machine rockets us through storms, crashes, earthquakes, I don't know what, really—I slept the entire two hundred kilometers, except for a couple of times when the man on my left, a Congolese youth named Max, woke me to complain I was drooling on his shoulder. The trip ended at the mission's church in Bunia, where those of us with religion went inside, and the two lost souls, Michael and I, stood under the awning of a cycle shop, trying to carve a plan out of the rain.

You have to remember, Tina, that the end wasn't yet, that all I had was Michael Adriko, meaning all I had was bitterness and doubt—and 68 hours to make the next 4800 kilometers.

Michael said, "Let's wear collars, you and I."

"Dog collars? Do I look like a dog?"

"Clerical collars."

"Do I look like a clerk?"

"I think it would help with questions."

"It's a lousy cover. Everyone wants to approach you."

"Who approached those Adventist people? We moved right through the checkpoints."

"I wouldn't know," I admitted. "I was asleep. But are you serious?"

"It's a joke. Come on, smile."

"I hate it when people tell me to smile. People like that disgust me."

"Nair, I have a bit of news: tomorrow afternoon we'll board a plane for Accra. We'll land in Kotoka International by next day's dawning."

"I don't believe you. Is that a surprise?"

"You'll believe me before too much longer. And then when I tell you to smile, you'll smile."

We passed the night at Le Citizen Hôtel, mostly in the café, where we sent out for fresh clothes, and where Michael got me drunk enough to promise I'd drink no more if we reached Freetown in time to make my rendezvous—still about sixty hours distant, and still no closer on the map. Therefore, I gave him my promise . . . The room we took came with its own sink. I vomited in it.

The next morning I lay in bed resting, or dying, while Michael went out to trip a lever, or touch a magic eye—in retrospect it looks that simple, the work of a finger—to set going his plan for extraction.

Even now, as I write this, with everything, or a good bit of everything, having turned out all right, I feel irritated with Michael's coy dramatics. I'm forced to give him credit, I admit that gratefully. We've crawled from the wreck, we've walked away, and all of that is Michael's doing. I'd just sort of rather it weren't.

At noon on Oct 29, with 52 hours to go, we hired a car with one of my twenty-dollar bills, and in thirty minutes we reached the checkpoint outside Bunia's airfield.

A guard in khaki peered inside the car, had us step out a minute, waved his wand at us, ignored its squeaks, then prodded aside a couple of goats with his boot and unhooked a rope to let us through.

Three flagpoles, two drooping flags, a red dirt runway. A concrete kiosk. In front of it some men in uniform loitered, laughing. Nothing else but a sort of restaurant with a wooden porch. I said, "I don't see any planes."

"Do you see those Ghanaian uniforms?"

"I see uniforms."

"Ghanaian. Wait here. But first give me money."

"How much?"

"Everything. If we want to get out of here, we have to pay."

He left me in the café. I found nobody inside. There were some tables and a cold-box full of drinks—unplugged—but nothing zestier than Coke. I guzzled a warm one. Michael joined me after ten minutes. He sat down without a drink and said, "When we get to Accra, I'll leave you at the airport terminal while I get the Ghanaian passports."

"Wonderful."

"You want diplomatic, or private?"

"One of each. And while you're about it, get me a medical diploma."

"I'm glad you don't believe me. It heightens the enjoyment later."

"Care to reveal how we get there?"

"Where?"

"Accra, Goddamn it."

"Ghanaian Air Force, flying for the UN."

"The UN? Their planes are never on time."

"You're very negative. Here's one hundred eighty dollars back. The pilots were reasonable in their requirements."

At Kotoka International in Accra, he handed me a cube of Big G Original Gum in a red wrapper and said, "Here, keep yourself busy," and next he went into the city and accomplished the unthinkable—although by then I was allowing myself to think it, because he'd gotten us this far, and because two Ghanaian thugs wearing dark business suits came in a Mercedes to collect him at the terminal.

That's where I sat for the next many hours—fifteen, I believe—until Michael returned around 11 that night.

He found me at the Teatime Kiosk at Kotoka, where I happened to be writing my last communication to you, Davidia, or to you, Tina, or to both of you . . . He laid out on the tabletop four Ghanaian documents, a pair of them for each of us—one a civilian passport, and the other a diplomatic, both stamped with visas for Sierra Leone, Uganda, and Liberia. "I started to come for you, to get your photo snapped—but there was a fellow there, an English, who looked just like you. A perfect double. He agreed to substitute."

"This doesn't look at all like me."

"It looks like you exactly," Michael insisted.

"Of course it does. To an African."

I can't tell you my name, Tina. But don't ask for Roland Nair.

"I'm born in Kumasi, and you in Accra. Both of us on the same day, because we're brothers."

"But I didn't give you any money."

Apparently he'd paid none. "I told you—I saved the president's life. I've told you many times."

"I don't remember any such lie. President who? Mahama? Is that his name?"

"No. It was in 2005. President John Kufuor. When we have privacy, I'll open my pants for you."

"What-what?"

"I took a bullet for him. I'll show you the scar."

At six the following morning, October 31st, we boarded a Kenya Airlines flight to Lungi International in Freetown.

The whole trip, from the sorrows of Newada Mountain to the comfort of the National Pride Suites, took 71 hours.

On the plane I said something which, though it came from my own mouth, I could scarcely believe: "Michael, if we don't crash, I'll make it on time. We'll get to Freetown with five hours to spare."

It didn't matter that a swarm of unforeseeables waited ahead, that anything could sink us. To be back in the running felt like triumph.

"How much for your enterprise?"

"What?"

"How much will you profit, Nair, how much money?"

"One hundred K US. That's the price for betraying absolutely everyone."

"But, Nair—you didn't betray me."

"Not quite. Not yet."

"The slate is clean between us."

"I tried to steal your girl."

"I take it as a compliment."

When we landed here in Freetown, Michael took a car to the National and I took another, first to the Paradi Restaurant for the briefest and happiest of errands—retrieving a bit of computer equipment—and then to the Bawarchi, where I waited until my friend Hamid arrived with one hundred thousand dollars in a blue plastic pouch with a zipper. I held the money in my lap while he used his own computer to examine the goods, and then we parted ways. No handshake. But if the chance comes again, I think we'll do business.

Late last night Michael and I met with some men in the bar downstairs and arranged to hire a boat, a big one. Experienced captain, plenty of fuel, and next stop—anywhere. Abidjan, perhaps. Though neither of us has much French.

Meanwhile we'll confine ourselves to this building, because too many people know Michael by sight. We share a suite of two rooms. The air conditioner and TV seldom work—no generator at the National—so it's hot, and it's boring. This afternoon for entertainment I watched Michael cut the stitches in his arm with barber scissors and pull them out with his teeth.

We'll wait till after midnight to break camp.

Maybe Liberia. Much is possible there. We'll claim a patch of jungle and a strip of beach, and I'll start my semi-honest account while Michael maps out a scheme or two for international conquest.

We don't have to put down roots. Maybe we'll keep moving. Michael and I both liked Uganda. Why not? The climate's pleasant.

When I left him two hours ago, Michael was downstairs in the bar, bent over a bulky very out-of-date video game machine, saying to it, "Pchew! Pchew! Pchew! In yo face, outa space!"

For him, Davidia, you were simply Fiancée Number Five. But for me. Good Lord. For me.

Tina, you more than once predicted that the coldness of my heart would someday make you a bitter woman. I think you chose me for exactly that reason. You must have wanted it. If you're bitter, you devised to become that way, and I think you chose me as your instrument. So stop it. Stop going on and on about it in my mind.

Maybe back to Ghana. Maybe Senegal. There's always Cameroon.

Or we might leave this continent behind us and fly to Kuwait, where Michael counts on a most enthusiastic welcome, having once, he revealed to me this morning, spent several months reorganizing and polishing every aspect of personal security for that country's emir, Sheikh Sabah IV Al-Ahmad Al-Jaber Al-Sabah, "thus prolonging his joy for many years."

I'm inclined to believe it.